MOON WARLORDS

Wilson Foo Yu Kang

Contents

I.   Arrival

"Aren't you excited? We're landing in less than half an hour!" exclaimed Kail, after hearing the announcement broadcast over the intercom of the space shuttle.

"It's not my first trip to the moon, Kail," replied his companion, "And it's not such fun once you get there. Everything in domes and tunnels, no going out in the open air. Well, there is no open air."

Chandor listened to the conversation beside him with some amusement. It was his first trip to the moon, too. He wasn't as excited as Kail was, but he was looking forward to being on the moon with some interest. He had been researching about moving to the moon for almost a year before he decided to buy a 1 way ticket, pack up and leave for the moon.

There was so much Chandor was leaving behind, but he was glad to be having a fresh start. Too much baggage back home had left him feeling too emotionally encumbered to continue staying where he was. Fresh from a breakup and somewhat estranged from his relations, Chandor had little he missed back home.

"Look, Nith, we can see the earth as a crescent like it's the moon!" said Kail.

Chandor looked toward the window. Indeed, it was a sight to behold. One knew that the earth was round, but it never appeared so while one was on the earth. So close to the moon, the earth became the moon, albeit a much more colourful one, with white clouds swirling above a miasma of green and blue.

The steward came by at that moment to serve their final snack. Only their first meal had been usual earth fare. Now that they were in orbit, they had to eat space food. Chandor did not like the freeze-dried confections, all of which seemed to taste the same. He was not looking forward to a lifetime of space food on the moon, but he would have to get used to it in time. That was the trade off for going to the moon and getting a new start.

Chandor opened his packet, labeled "Chicken Pie". He could use the water guns in front of his seat to rehydrate it with either cold or hot water, but he decided not to do so after his last attempt with apple pie, which ended up soggy and tasting like sugar syrup. He bit into the crunchy hard foam. At least it had some taste, even if it just tasted like salty foam. He had heard that once on the moon, though, there was slightly better space food which could be prepared as there was some gravity there, as opposed to the complete zero gravity environment in the space shuttle.

In about 15 minutes, Chandor finished his chicken-pie-flavoured foam. The intercom buzzed, signaling another announcement.

"Ladies & gentlemen, this is your captain speaking. We will be landing in 15 minutes. Please ensure all your personal belongings are fastened to avoid them floating away. Ensure that you place the anti-bacterial tablet into your food packages after consuming them to prevent bacterial growth in the spacecraft."

In no time, the spacecraft left the moon's orbit and started spiralling down towards its surface.

"My first view of the moon up close!" exclaimed Kail, ever excited.

"A lot less colourful than earth. Literally," remarked his companion, Nith, drily.

Chandor looked out the window into the blackness of space and the greyness of moon dust. Indeed, the moon's surface didn't look like much from up close, although there seemed to be hills and valleys. Certainly, a far cry from the bright and vibrant forests and oceans of earth. Well, there would be colour and light once he was inside the tunnels and domes of the moon. All of which, of course, was man-made. Well, that was the price to pay for wanting a fresh start.

The shuttle began to vibrate as it docked into the spaceport. After what seemed like an aeon of whirring noises, the shuttle stopped moving. Chandor realised that he actually felt like he was sitting on his seat - rather than like he was being held in by the strap. Gravity had kicked in again on the moon's surface, although he felt really light.

"Ladies & gentlemen, thank you for travelling with the Alexis space shuttle service. We have docked at Lintal spaceport. We wish you a pleasant stay on the moon," came the final announcement as all the passengers on board the shuttle began taking off their seat belts and retrieving their baggage. Chandor was travelling light and had only a large haversack with him, most of his belongings being scheduled to arrive via a cargo shuttle later on. He pulled his backpack from the receptacle under his seat, slung it on his shoulders and stood up.

"Ow!"

Unexpectedly, a cry came from beside him.

"Careful there, the gravity on the moon is one sixth of earth's," said Nith to Kail, chuckling.

Kail had hit his head on the ceiling standing up too suddenly. Chandor was glad he had his heavy backpack on, which had kept him on the ground. Well, it was supposed to be heavy - it felt incredibly light on the moon.

Chandor walked along the aisle of the spacecraft, feeling almost as if he was jumping with each step. He could see Kail walking gingerly in the next aisle, careful not to hit the ceiling again.

"Thank you for flying with us, sir." An attendant greeted Chandor as he walked out of the spacecraft.

As Chandor disembarked from the spacecraft, he saw what a spaceport on the moon looked like for the first time. It looked very similar to an airport, but smaller and more cramped. The ceilings all looked curved and rounded. He guessed that it was due to the system of domes and tunnels on the moon. Chandor got on a travelator and headed towards immigration.

After Chandor got his iris scanned by the immigration machine, he made for the exit of the spaceport. However, scanning the area, he could not seem to find one.

"Hey man, you look lost," said a voice from behind him.

He turned around to look. It was Kail, who sat beside him on the spacecraft.

"Yeah, you're right, I am. How do I get out of the spaceport?"

"You can't! If you did you'd be dead. Well, unless you're going on a moonwalk," replied Kail.

"Right, I've forgotten that we're on the moon and there's no going out. It's my first time here. You too, right?"

"Yeah, same here, though at least I've got Nith here with me," Kail gestured to Nith, standing beside him.

"Where are you headed?" asked Nith.

"I bought a place in Lintal, here's the address." Chandor showed Nith the address:

Lintal, Avked Quarter, Trij Network, Tube 5, Dome 20, Unit B3-25

"Wow, you bought a property, and it's your first time on the moon? You must be rich as Croesus," remarked Kail.

"Nope, I sold my home on earth. I'm moving here for good," replied Chandor.

Nith gave a low whistle. "A brave soul, this one. Have you even heard about what the situation on the moon is like?"

"I hear it's a bit dicey now, but Lintal's safe. At least as far as the political system is concerned," answered Chandor. "Why? What's wrong with things on the moon now?"

"I wouldn't dare to stay on the moon, and I've been here several times on business trips already. To say it's dicey doesn't even begin to describe what's been going on for the past decade. Lintal's at peace, or so they say, but it's a delicate peace. The moon's no longer the united place it once was. I mean, of course, you know there are now 3 factions on the moon, Lintal, Blissaune and Clidurna. The situation's anything but stable. They're doing everything they can to gain power over the others, short of outright war - that would kill everyone. I wouldn't come here if I had a choice. You never know what might happen to you," Nith responded in a low voice.

"Well, this spaceport looks peaceful enough," mused Chandor.

"We'd better help him get where he's going, hadn't we? We haven't got all day. Is it on our way, Nith?" Kail chimed in.

"It's not exactly on the way, but we can make a slight detour to help our new friend. Our meetings only start tomorrow anyway. We can hop on an express travellator; it's some distance away from here."

"Lead the way, Nith!" went Kail gaily.

Nith led them down a maze of travellators in a series of hallways. *I'll get lost easily*, thought Chandor. "It's like everything's in the same building. It never ends," Chandor thought aloud.

"Yeah, I know, right? It's like one of those underground shopping malls on earth that go for miles and miles. But this goes on forever," said Kail.

They reached a nexus of many travellators, some of which people walked on, and some of which had tiny capsules which people sat in.

"We're getting on this one." Nith pointed to a travellator with a sign above it that said Trij

Network. The travellator had capsules moving on it, and was not level with the ground - it led into a curved tunnel that curved upward, out of the roof of the dome that they were currently in. It looked like a roller coaster. Another sign, below the one that said Trij Network, showed, "1 minute waiting time".

Soon, the ground in front of them opened up, revealing a small empty capsule which could fit 4 people that moved up slowly to ground level. The sign now read "Ready for next 4 passengers", and an intercom announced the same. Nith stepped up to the capsule and placed his finger on a fingerprint sensor.

"3 LDR deducted," a voice sounded from the capsule.

"We've got to pay for this?" asked Kail.

"The company's paying for our transport, but our friend here has got to pay his own way. He can afford it, he's got a house over here so he's certainly got LDR."

"Yes, I do." Chandor scanned his fingerprint. "3 LDR deducted," the capsule sounded again.

Kail followed suit. They climbed into the capsule and buckled up their seat belts.

"What's LDR again? I forgot," asked Kail.

"Lintal Drawing Rights," replied Chandor. It was one of the few things he knew about the moon, as he had to exchange his US dollars for LDRs before he bought his property on the moon. It was a unique name for a currency, leading Chandor to do some research on it. The moon, originally a single political entity, used to have the Special Drawing Rights used by the International Monetary Fund on earth as its currency. After it splintered into territories controlled by 3 factions, Lintal kept the name "Drawing Rights" for its currency, while the other 2 factions adopted different names for their currencies.

"Is there a 4th person?" the capsule sounded. A screen at the front of the capsule showed the question and 2 buttons, "Yes" and "No". "I don't think we want to wait for a 4th person just so we can save 1 LDR each," said Nith, "So we're just going to go ahead." Nith tapped "No".

"Fee adjusted to 4 LDR per passenger. 5, 4, 3, 2, 1," sounded the capsule, and they were off, zooming up into the sky. The roof of the tunnel was made of a transparent material and they could see the stars up above.

"Beautiful!" exclaimed Kail. "This is a nice touch. I thought everything would be covered up just like in the spaceport."

"Yes, the stars are really clear here. It must be the lack of an atmosphere," Chandor joined in.

"By the way, I never got your name," said Kail.

"I'm Chandor. And I know, you're Kail and Nith. I overheard your names on the space shuttle."

"And what line might you be in?"

"I haven't got a job now, since I quit my job to move to the moon. But I used to be a chemical engineer."

"Whoa! Heard that, Nith? We could really use somebody like him!"

"Oh, why? What do you guys do?"

"We're freeze-dried food importers. Really big stuff. The moon depends on the earth completely for its food supply. We supply produce to almost half the eateries on Lintal. Well, you know what freeze-dried food tastes like. You've had it on the space shuttle. Not great. It's a little better here because they have technicians who can hydrate your food with just the right amounts of hot water or cold water for you, but it's still not something anyone really wants to eat. So we're constantly on the lookout for chemical engineers who can develop better ways of freeze drying food so it at least becomes something palatable. Even if it doesn't really taste like the original."

"Oh, I didn't really do that sort of chemical engineering. Not into food related stuff, actually."

"What sort of chemical engineering do you do then?"

"Industrial substances. Most of the time they're really toxic stuff. Not stuff you'd want to eat." Chandor gave a slight smile.

"Eek." Kail made a face. "Doesn't sound fun."

"I'm hoping to do something different on the moon, though. Not sure what yet," added Chandor, "I'm going to take maybe a month or 2 to find out. Probably going to explore Lintal a fair bit as well, seeing as I'm new here."

The capsule slowed down to a stop. "You have arrived at your destination," sounded the capsule.

Chandor, Kail and Nith climbed out of the capsule to behold yet another intersection of several travelators, most of them without capsules this time. "Now, we've got to get to dome 20 along tube 5. I think it's this travelator. It says tube 5, right here." Nith pointed to one of the travelators.

They hopped on. After passing several domes, the sign Dome 20 finally appeared on the wall.

"Well, there you go. Dome 20." Nith smiled at Chandor. "Need us to go along with you to find your unit?"

"Yeah, sounds like a good idea, I don't want to lose my way."

Nith took out his communicator, a tiny button which he held in his hand and pressed to unlock its screen. He gestured in the air and a holographic map appeared.

"Now, it looks like there's an elevator which takes you right to your door just behind this wall." They went around the wall, saw the elevator and got in. "Unit B3-25," Chandor said, before the elevator could ask.

"Right away, sir," the elevator revved into motion and in a few seconds, opened at the doorway to Unit B3-25.

"So convenient to have elevators that go to every unit. On earth there are so many buildings with vertical-only elevators because those old buildings can't be upgraded to accomodate vertical-horizontal elevators," remarked Chandor.

"Well, this is the moon." Nith gestured with an expansive sweep of his arm. "Everything was built according to plan. Well, at least it once was when humans first settled the moon. You know, that's what they said Australia's capital city Canberra was like when it was first built.

Everything according to plan. Now you see the typical urban sprawl everywhere. It's harder to have urban sprawl on the moon because you can't just go somewhere and pitch a tent, for instance, you wouldn't have air to breathe until the ducts are built and all that."

"Yup. Same, same, but different." Chandor scanned his fingerprint on the door and the door opened to reveal a garishly coloured apartment inside. "Thanks for bringing me home; I wouldn't know what I would've done without you guys. Won't you folks come in for a drink?"

"Well, it's late. We might not have days and nights on the moon, or at least day and night never change depending on where you are, but we still run according to earth time. We'd better get going. Perhaps you can catch us for a drink sometime," said Nith.

"Let's exchange contacts!" said Kail. He took out his communicator and so did Chandor and Nith. "There!" Kail, Chandor and Nith touched their communicators together. "Contacts shared," the 3 communicators sounded together.

"Well, we'll catch you sometime. Have a good one." Nith waved goodbye as he and Kail left.

II.   Settling in

Chandor laid his haversack down and closed the door. The apartment was brightly coloured in cyan, magenta and yellow, almost like a children's playground. *Must be to make up for the lack of colour outside*, he thought. He had not selected a design for his apartment when he bought it, deciding to leave it to chance. This would take some getting used to.

Thirsty, Chandor decided to get some water. He looked around the house for a kitchen. Finding no place that looked like a kitchen, he wondered how he would get water. Then, he saw 2 water guns in the hall, mounted at the side of the wall, along with 2 cups. *Makes sense*, he thought, *they can't cook anything here, they can only rehydrate freeze-dried food. Doesn't stand to reason that there would be a kitchen*. He pointed the water gun labeled cold into one of the cups and fired. Not realising that the trigger was pressure sensitive, he pressed it too hard and the water hit the bottom of the cup and bounced back out again, spraying droplets everywhere.

"Gah!" exclaimed Chandor as the water droplets slowly descended to the ground. This was going to be even more difficult to clean up than a spillage on earth, where the water at least pooled quickly on a surface. Here, they were so light they fell slowly like snowflakes.

Chandor gave up on the cup and squirted water directly from the water gun into his mouth instead. His thirst quenched, he set out to clean up the spillage. He took some tissue from his haversack and slowly, carefully, gathered up the water droplets. Finally, the mess was cleaned up and he disposed of the tissue.

Chandor looked around his new home. The hall had a small sofa for lounging, in bright, garish magenta. There were some yellow chairs and a cyan table. There was a small rug in front of the sofa, which said "Home Sweet Home" in multiple colours. He headed to the only room in the house. In the room was a bed, in similarly bright colours, with two fastening straps to hold the sleeper down while sleeping, in case any moonquakes caused the sleeper to fly off the bed. There was a single cupboard, which was empty except for a new spacesuit and its attached oxygen tank. A sign hung on the spacesuit which read, "Do not use until you have read the manual in full".

"Now that's something," remarked Chandor to himself. He took a look at the restroom. In contrast to the rest of the house, it was plainly coloured, most of it in shades of cream and off-white. Perhaps the designers felt that the colour had to signal that the restroom was different from the rest of the house. There were no taps, but instead, 2 water guns, warm and cold, above the basin. The toilet did not appear to have a flushing cistern above the seat. Chandor pressed the flush button and was rewarded with suction noise from the toilet bowl, with some liquid chemical, probably disinfectant, released therein.

Kind of like an airplane toilet, he thought. He went back to the sofa and pressed his communicator button. A holographic screen appeared in front of him.

"Good day, sir. What can we do for you today?"

"What's the latest news on Lintal?"

The screen changed to show the news for the day. Somebody hacking into a bank's systems and squirrelling away money here, a traffic jam on the travelators there, everything seemed as mundane as it was on earth. Then something caught his eye:

"Suspected operative from Blissaune under investigation for sabotage of air vents."

Chandor looked more intently and the communicator caught his intention. It magnified the article and started playing the video associated with it.

"A 32-year-old man, suspected to be an operative from Blissaune, has been arrested for alleged sabotage of the air vents leading to the President's chambers. Blissaune has verified that the unidentified man is one of its citizens, but has vehemently denied that it had sanctioned any sabotage. Blissaune's foreign minister said that it would be providing consular assistance to the man and emphasised that under Lintal's laws, the man is innocent until proven guilty. Military Intelligence of Lintal revealed that it has thus far uncovered evidence of what it believes to be a network of operatives working under Blissaune's instructions to commence a campaign of covert sabotage against Lintal. Blissaune has claimed that MIL's comments are unhelpful and have a tendency to destabilise the already rocky relations between the 3 localities of the moon," read the newscaster, with footage of a man being handcuffed in the background.

Dicey, thought Chandor, *I'd better look out and hotfoot it to somewhere else if things heat up between Lintal and Blissaune.*

The rest of the news was unremarkable and Chandor browsed through it quickly. He yawned. The journey through space had tired him out. He went to shower and lay down on his bed, then he was soon fast asleep.

The next few days passed in a blur for Chandor as he explored his neighbourhood. It took some getting used to as there were no roads like on earth, only travelators, and everything was essentially in the same building. Once you got on the wrong travelator, there was sometimes no easy way back and sometimes you had to make a major detour even to go to someplace nearby.

He tried some of the eateries, including those which had water-gun rehydration experts and unique flavours of freeze-dried food, but all of the rehydrated freeze-dried food still tasted like salted slush to him. He decided to simply eat freeze-dried food from the convenience store without rehydrating it, like a biscuit. Some of the desserts actually tasted like meringues that way, which was not too bad.

After a while, he began to know his immediate neighbourhood pretty well. He was initially a little unused to the apartments all being like rooms in a hotel, along long corridors, but interspersed with shops, information counters, offices and other units.

Chandor went for his first moon walk as well. It was a surreal experience as he put on the spacesuit, then was taken out of the dome in a special lift. Stepping on the moon's soil and looking at his bootprint was fun for a while. After a while, however, the terrain of the moon looked the same everywhere - hills of fine grey dust, among which human tunnels and domes were built. The tunnels and domes didn't look like much from the outside either, as there were no lights. There was no sunlight, and all Chandor could see was what the flashlight on his spacesuit could illuminate. It got old after a while.

About 5 days after his arrival, Chandor got a call on his communicator.

"Show caller," he commanded.

Kail's face appeared in a holographic screen in front of him.

"Hey man, how's it going settling down in your new place?"

"Not too bad, I've gone for a moonwalk."

"Sounds fab, I haven't even had the time to go for one myself. So, shall we go get that drink soon? We've got something that may interest you. We're leaving for earth pretty soon so you gotta be quick."

"Something that may interest me? Like what?"

"Something involving chemical engineering. Let you know more when we meet. Can you meet tomorrow?"

"Sure, where and when?"

"Let's do Lune Lodge. That's pretty close to where you are. 2:00 PM GMT." Hearing the abbreviation for Greenwich Mean Time struck Chandor as somewhat odd given that they were on the moon, but the moon followed earth time, since there was no real day and night on the moon.

"Yes, it's close by. See you and Nith then!"

The next day, Chandor set out from his home to Lune Lodge. It was one of the few bars that actually served alcohol, an expensive commodity on the moon as it had to be processed by converting it into a special powder, which took up huge amounts of energy. Chandor figured it was worth the price to find out what Kail and Nith had in mind.

When he arrived, Kail and Nith were already there at a table in the corner. Kail waved him over. "Over here, mate!"

Chandor headed over.

"Great, what are you getting? We've ordered already."

Chandor glanced at the menu. "I guess I'll have Moonshake Madness. Sounds good and I haven't had it before."

"Good choice," said Nith approvingly.

Their drinks came soon.

"There's no kick in these drinks at all. They put so little alcohol in them, not like on earth," complained Kail.

"Alcohol's expensive here, it's more for the novelty factor," reminded Nith, "You pretty much can't get drunk anywhere on the moon. This place is as good as any. Now, to our friend Chandor finally settling down on the moon. Cheers."

They clinked their glasses together and each took a sip of their drinks.

"So what's this secretive hush hush business you've got for me?" asked Chandor.

"Well, see, we just supplied food to a major manufacturer here on the moon. He's not from Lintal. He's Clidurnian," replied Kail.

"Refresh my memory again. The 3 factions on the moon are?"

"Lintal, Clidurna and Blissaune. They differ in political systems. Lintal is a presidential republic, Clidurna is a parliamentary democracy and Blissaune is an absolute monarchy."

"Right, I knew that." Chandor gave a wan smile.

"So, the rumour's out that things are not going well between Lintal and Blissaune. Clidurna's peaceful and our customer is into a huge line of business there. He's not into food, he orders food from us only because he provides food for his staff. He's into defence related stuff. He can't exactly tell us what it is, but it's something to do with research into novel substances that can be found on the moon. Then they see if there's a way to create something useful out of that."

"Right, and how do I fit into all of this?" asked Chandor.

"He's thinking of hiring a chemical engineer soon. They have a secret project. Something that might need your expertise."

"What sort of secret project?"

"It's secret, obviously I don't know." Kail sounded exasperated. "But what I do know is that they harvest copious amounts of moon dust. As far as I know, Lintal and Blissaune largely see moon dust as useless. Not Clidurna. There's a huge market there for moon dust. God knows what they do with it. And our customer's into moon dust in a big way. He's got a whole fleet of remote controlled robots which harvest moon dust and bring it back to his refinery in Clidurna. Dangerous stuff, too - I heard you can get a way more severe form of hay fever if you inhale moon dust."

"And you thought I would be interested because…" Chandor raised an eyebrow.

"You told us yourself, you worked in industrial substances before. Toxic stuff, you said. I don't know about you, but moon dust sounds like it could be right up your alley in that case."

"I just bought a house in Lintal, you know. I've just uprooted myself from earth. And now you're asking me to uproot myself again?"

Nith interjected. "Look, Chandor, things are not what they once were. Things are afoot between Lintal and Blissaune. Nasty things. You might think you're not messing with anybody, but that's not gonna cut it. Other people will come messing with you, even if you're not doing them any harm. Stay in Lintal too long, and the least that could happen is that your property will be worthless. I don't even want to imagine what's the worst possibility. You've gotta think of getting out while the going's good. Even if you've just arrived."

Chandor took a sip of his drink. *This is all coming a bit too soon*, he thought, *I've just moved here and I was hoping to have some peace and quiet for a bit, and now they're asking me to leave this place.*

"Well, I don't see the harm in exploring my options, seeing as I haven't got a job right now yet. So how do I get in touch with this guy?" asked Chandor.

"Say the word, and we'll take you there. Right now," said Kail, "'cuz we're not gonna be staying on the moon for much longer. Got stuff to do back on earth."

"Now? I'm not even dressed for an interview." Chandor was wearing a t-shirt and a pair of shorts, "I thought we were just going to have drinks and chill out."

"Nobody dresses up for an interview on the moon, Chandor. Or for work either. Since the temperature's controlled and the weather's the same all year round anyway, everyone dresses just like you're dressed now. Look at us, we just came from a work meeting," said Nith. Nith was dressed in a t-shirt and shorts as well, as was Kail.

"Right, so I guess you've got to tell your mysterious customer I'm going to meet him?"

"Yup, just a minute." Nith pressed his communicator. "Get me Thurl," he commanded.

After the communicator rang a few times, a heavyset man appeared in front of them.

"Hey, how's it going? I see you've got company with you."

Chandor waved. "Nice to see you too."

"You must be Chandor."

"Got that right."

"I'm Thurl. So, Kail and Nith must have told you about me?"

"Well, they told me about the job opportunity you have for me."

"Great. Now I'm a bit of a dinosaur where interviews are concerned and I don't like to conduct them over the communicator. Have you decided that you'd like to come and see me in person?"

"Yes, we were just talking about that. I'll come and see you. I haven't got a job yet anyway."

"Great. I'm going to head over to Krid network in Larkt quarter over in Lintal then. That's near the border to Clidurna. I'll see you in about an hour or so then?"

"Sure thing," Kail chimed in. The communicator went off.

"I don't know what I'm getting myself into. I've just met you guys a couple of days ago and now I'm meeting Thurl for the first time. Being on the moon sure is fast paced," said Chandor.

"No time like the present. Live in the moment, Chandor. You jettisoned everything on earth to come here, what else have you got to lose?" said Nith.

"Right you are."

Kail, Nith and Chandor finished their drinks and in no time, they were on the travelators again. It was the afternoon according to GMT time, but as they looked out of the transparent ceiling from their capsule on another high speed travelator, they saw stars.

"I've got to get used to this. It's night all the time."

"Whaddya expect, Lintal's on the dark side of the moon. But actually, the dark side of the moon gets sunlight, though I won't be around to experience it," said Kail.

"There's sunlight on the dark side of the moon? Why's it called the dark side, then?" Chandor did not remember what he read about this.

"It's called the dark side because it faces away from earth, so it used to be the unknown side of the moon before humans came and settled here. But yes, it gets sunlight. The bright side gets 2 weeks of sunlight, then the dark side gets 2 weeks in turn. But the bright side also gets earthlight, which is reflected sunlight from the earth, even when it doesn't get sunlight, so it's always day there, only that it becomes twilight when it's a lunar eclipse. The bright side is truly the bright side. The dark side is dark in the sense that it actually gets dark for 2 weeks at a time."

"Wow, you know a lot, fellow first timer on the moon," remarked Chandor.

"You bet. I was so excited to come. I read up all about the moon before I came. I read all the legends on earth about people imagining fairies on the moon and stuff and I read the moon's ancient history on the first lunar landings by the Apollo spacecraft." Kail gave Chandor a smug look.

"Pity you're going back to earth so soon, then."

"I know, right? We should've extended our stay here, go for a holiday or something. But Nith says we're coming back again. I'm looking forward to it, he isn't."

"You'll feel the same way after you've been to the moon as many times as I have. Earth sweet earth," sighed Nith.

After some time, the capsule sounded, "You have arrived at your destination." Kail, Nith and Chandor got out of the capsule. Then followed another maze of travelators before they arrived at Krid network.

"We forgot to ask him where we'd be meeting." Nith pulled out his communicator button. "Let me check."

"Get me Thurl," he commanded.

The communicator rang a few times, then Thurl's face appeared.

"Are you guys there already?" Thurl asked.

"We're at Krid network. Where should we meet you?" Nith responded.

"I'm at Krid network too. Seeing as you're a bunch of earthlings, let's go to Just Like On Earth. It's an eatery. Tube 3, Dome 10, Unit B2-47. See you there."

Nith led the way down a few corridors before they found the place. The moment they opened the doors, a wonderful smell wafted from out of the kitchen.

"Wow, this is amazing! What's that?"

"Told you. Just Like On Earth. Name says it all," boomed a voice from behind them.

"Thurl!" Nith exclaimed.

"Wow, this must cost a bomb," remarked Kail.

"Nothing to worry about, folks. This one's on me. I've made a reservation." Thurl scanned his fingerprint at a counter on the wall labeled "Reservations". "Table 9," the machine sounded as a holographic image displaying "Table 9" appeared above one of the tables in the corner, cordoned off from the next table by a partition.

"I picked a spot where we might have a tad more privacy, even though that's still a bit difficult," Thurl said as he walked towards table 9. The rest followed him.

Chandor looked at the menu. He was surprised that it listed ordinary food that one could have on earth. "Wow, steak?"

"Yes. This is a new experimental place. The food's still dehydrated, of course, but they've got an amazing new rehydration machine. It's not water guns. And the food's not foam. It's basically dried meat and other real food from earth. Really really expensive and difficult to bring in."

"Must really cost a bomb, like Kail said," remarked Chandor, "You're pulling out all the stops for me, huh?"

"You're real quick to catch on, Chandor." Thurl smiled. *Did that smile appear a little sinister, or was that just me?* thought Chandor.

They ordered their food, Chandor having steak, Thurl having fish, Kail having chicken and Nith having squid.

"Wow, this actually tastes like beef, even though it's a bit tough." Chandor said in between chews. "Anyone want to try?"

They all shared a bit of each other's food and agreed that while it still tasted a bit preserved and artificial, this was the best food they'd had on the moon yet.

"And you guys are the ones from Lintal! Shame on you that you didn't know about this place," said Thurl.

"Hey, we're not really from Lintal. We don't live on the moon, well, except for Chandor here who's new. We just come here and do the same thing every time. Besides, we're food suppliers. Can't let others know there's food that's better than our own," Nith responded.

"Why do you still get food from them if this is so much better?" Chandor joked.

"I'd be broke in a second if I had this all the time," rejoined Thurl, "Besides, I'm used to moon food. Not like you earthlings."

"So, let's talk about what we're here for. Apart from the excellent food. You wanted to interview me," reminded Chandor.

"Yes, and I'd like to know if you're up to the mark for what we need. Basically, we need a chemical engineer who specialises in the manufacture of substances and has experience in handling toxic materials. Tell me, Chandor, what's your experience?"

"Well, I've dealt with all sorts of hazardous stuff back on earth. Asbestos, flammable liquids, the like. I've done manufacturing and I've done safety monitoring too. But I've no experience with what you're handling here, though. Kail says you deal in moon dust?"

"That's one of the major things we do. See, moon dust is seen by most people as a pesky irritant. It gums up spacesuits, for instance - it's like glass so when it gets into the joints of spacesuits, it melts then it solidifies and jams the movement of the spacesuit. Could be fatal."

"Silicon dioxide." Chandor nodded.

"Yes, which brings me to another of the hazards of moon dust. Silicosis. Breathing it in kills you slowly and painfully. That's why every lift to the surface has a triple airlock that cleans the dust off your spacesuit everytime you return from a moonwalk," Thurl continued.

"But we see the potential in moon dust. There's a lot of use for moon dust that only Clidurna has discovered. We keep these discoveries hush hush because of their sheer economic, and even military potential. If Lintal or Blissaune were to get wind of this, we'd lose out competitive advantage in an instant, and might even be in mortal danger. Especially Blissaune. At least Lintal and Clidurna are democracies, but Blissaune is an autocratic kingdom ruled with an iron fist."

Chandor nodded again. "I've done confidential government projects before. Nothing so secret as what you have, but they would've resulted in some degree of embarrassment to several of earth's governments if they'd been leaked. When I was on earth, I had a security clearance too. Those aren't given to everyone."

"Sounds impressive. So tell me about some of the projects you've done before as a chemical engineer. Just what you can tell me about, of course."

"Well, there was this project I did where we had to get rid of a whole load of toxic waste generated by a secret government project. Some fool had the bright idea of covering it all up by burying it in the ground. Radiation as well as toxins were leaching into the soil. The people living above it didn't know it was there; it had been deposited using a tunneling machine. Some environmentalist went to the site and found there was something amiss. If it had been discovered, there would've been a tremendous uproar.

So I was one of the team members tasked to find a solution quickly to get rid of the toxins and radiation before the dump could be exposed. It was a race against time. We didn't have any solution and basically sat there stumped for days on end. Then one day, we chanced upon the solution.

We analysed the soil again and discovered that there were two chemicals in the toxic waste which could react with each other, if only there was a suitable catalyst. So we set about finding a catalyst. Indeed, we found one, after a lot of trial and error. Not only would the reaction neutralise the chemical properties of both chemicals, it would also generate a nuclear wave that would neutralise all the radioactivity of the rest of the waste.

We quickly got it mass produced and had a tunneling machine bore a tunnel to the toxic waste site underground, then injected the catalyst into the toxic waste. Thankfully, it worked. We saved the world, but nobody knew since we had to keep it secret.

Now, it sounds like I'm just proud of covering up an embarrassing episode for the government, but what I did really impacted lives. If we hadn't found a solution, who would've known what might've happened to the people living above all that waste?"

"Impressive, Chandor. Sounds like you and your team had a great deal of talent, coming up with a chemical like that in the nick of time. And you were very discreet as well. A lesser man would've leaked it to the public so he'd become a hero. But you and your team managed to keep it under wraps and preserve the peace."

"Thank you. I was doing my job."

"Well, Chandor, just based on that alone, I think we can offer you a job, with a probationary period of 1 month. That's if you want it. Nith says you mightn't want to move, given that you've just settled down in Lintal?" Thurl gave Chandor a quizzical look.

"Well, I've just uprooted myself from earth, and to uproot myself again so soon - my mind can't wrap itself around it."

"You know about the problems between Lintal and Blissaune, right? Lintal's not the safest place right now. Any moment now, things could erupt."

"Yes, it's really unexpected. I didn't think this would happen when I bought a house in Lintal while I was still on earth."

"Well, that's the moon for you. The new frontier. The Wild West, as they called it in the old days," Nith chimed in.

"So, how long do you need to think about it?" Thurl asked Chandor.

"Give me a day or two at least."

"Can do. Well, give me a ring, won't you? We've got to make special arrangements to transfer your moon residency to Clidurna. Citizenship laws on the moon are still in a state of flux and it's complicated."

III.   An unpleasant shock

Chandor returned home that night to have a sleepless night. He tossed and turned, weighing his options in his mind. *It's all going too fast*, he thought, *I just got here and now I've got to move?* Unable to get any sleep, he got up and decided to have a short walk outside. To his surprise, as soon as he opened his door, he saw multicoloured flashing lights and heard sirens going off outside. There appeared to be some sort of commotion.

"What's going on?" he asked one of the neighbours who was also standing outside his door.

"It's on the news. There's a suspected attack by Blissaune. And it's right in our dome," replied the neighbour.

Police were going about, questioning the people around.

"Have you seen anyone suspicious lately?" one of the police officers asked Chandor.

"Uh, no, uh…"

"Hey, I haven't seen this guy around before!" cried out another of the neighbours standing around outside.

"Yeah, come to think about it, neither have I," added the neighbour Chandor was talking to. "Who are you, man?"

"What's going on?" asked the police officer.

"I just came from Earth. I moved from Earth to Lintal. What's wrong?" asked Chandor.

"When was that?"

"Just a few days ago."

"Why'd you move to the moon? You got a job here?" The police officer sounded suspicious.

"No, I haven't got a job here. I just wanted to move to the moon."

"There's something fishy about this guy," chimed in one of the neighbours, "Appearing all of a sudden, and now there's sabotage in Lintal."

"You'd better investigate this guy," added the other neighbour.

"Hey, gimme a break, OK? Just because I'm the new kid on the block doesn't mean I'm a spy from Blissaune or whatever," rebutted Chandor.

"Folks, the police will decide what we wanna do. But you know what, I think we'd better ask you a few more questions. Come along with us," the police officer said to Chandor.

"What? What have I done?"

"If you haven't done anything at all, you've got nothing to fear." The police officer produced a tiny device which suddenly attracted both of Chandor's wrists and held them behind his back.

"Hey! Let me go!" Chandor exclaimed as he struggled to free his arms.

"I wouldn't try that if I were you. It can hurt. Besides, if you don't cooperate, I'm charging you with obstruction of justice. Come along with me to the station, now," the police officer ordered sternly.

Heart beating fast, Chandor followed the police officer. The suddenness of this unanticipated arrest left Chandor in shock.

At the station, Chandor was questioned by another police officer whom he presumed to be more superior.

"So, Chandor, is it? That's what it says in your ID. Or do you have another name?"

"Chandor it is," he replied.

"Why did you move to the moon all of a sudden?"

"I wanted a fresh start. I had a breakup. No close relations on earth."

"Any links to Blissaune?"

"No, I just got here."

An alert popped up at that moment. "Search complete," a voice said.

"Ah, now we'll see where our cameras have caught you the time you were here." A holographic image appeared in the air. "Let's see, now, who's this guy?" Thurl's face shone at Chandor.

"His name's Thurl. I don't know much about him. He's from Clidurna."

"A newcomer to the moon and you've already got friends from afar, haven't you? Don't know much about him, eh?"

"I just met him. He was recommended by 2 people who happened to be on the spacecraft I was in. He was trying to offer me a job in Clidurna."

"You expect me to believe that? You just happened to bump into 2 strangers on a spacecraft, who just happened to recommend you to somebody from Clidurna, and this Clidurnian just happened to offer you a job? Bit of a coincidence, isn't it?"

"Well, he's not from Blissaune. I'm telling you the truth. There isn't anyone from Clidurna suspected of any foul play in Lintal, is there?" asked Chandor.

"We can't exclude anyone. Blissaune's the prime suspect now, but who knows, Clidurna might be pulling the strings. You're certainly one of the more suspicious characters in Dome 20. Not the only one. But somebody like you, with few ties on the moon, no real reason to come here, and has connections with mysterious strangers, well, you bet we're going to be careful with you."

"So what happens to me now?"

"We have the power to hold you for investigation for 24 hours. 1 earth day. This is not earth, you don't have a right to a lawyer, not with moon politics being in the state of flux it's in right now. So you're gonna spend the night in the lockup while we decide what to do with you."

"Hey, I'm not a criminal. Why are you locking me up? What basis have you got?"

"Like I said, this is not earth. Security comes before human rights here. You stay put and don't cause any trouble and if our searches show that you're harmless as far as we know, we'll let you go, subject to more intense monitoring after you're released. Now, I'm done with you and I don't want any more questions." The interrogator left the room.

Another police officer brought Chandor to a cell. Unlike stereotypical jail cells on earth, this cell didn't have bars, and had smooth, curved walls everywhere. Its door was completely seamless and flush with the curved walls. If anything, it was probably harder to escape from than anything on earth.

Chandor sat on the bed in disbelief, wondering what he could do now. He could hardly comprehend how he had ended up here. The moon didn't seem to have any concept of legal rights. He was being arrested on nothing more than seeming vaguely suspicious, without any evidence that he had done anything at all. The fact that he had just arrived before being caught up in this whirlwind compounded his frustration and bewilderment. He pounded his fists on the bed in anger.

With nothing left to do, Chandor stared blankly ahead of him, unable to think of any way of getting himself out of his predicament. After some time, he realised it was futile being frustrated and decided to get some rest. He lay down on the bed and had a fitful sleep.

~

"Wake up. The officer in charge wants to see you," a voice boomed.

Chandor awoke with a start. He checked his watch. It had been 7 hours since he had fallen asleep.

The door to the cell opened. An officer came and led Chandor out, back to the room where he had been interrogated the day before.

"Your stay in our lovely hotel wasn't too hard on you, I hope?" The officer from the day before asked sarcastically.

"Well, I managed to get some sleep at least. No thanks to you folks."

"So, Chandor. Our searches have come in. It seems that nothing about you seems especially suspicious. That is, except the 2 strangers you met on the spacecraft and Thurl."

"What's suspicious about them?"

"We know Thurl's into moon dust. That's a very sensitive industry, if there ever was one. So he's probably not a simple character. Plus, we can't rule out the possibility that it might be Clidurna and not Blissaune which sabotaged us yesterday. Or maybe they're both in cahoots together," the officer continued, "The 2 people you talked to on the spacecraft also seem to be in some exotic line of business. And they're not from the moon - they're from earth. We're always careful about earthlings: who knows what links they might have? Yourself included."

"That's it? Just because they have a particular job and we're all not from Lintal? This is discrimination!" Chandor responded angrily.

"Like I told you yesterday, this is the moon. We're in a dicey situation. We haven't got time for all of your human rights nonsense. If you want rights, you go back to earth where you'll have them in spades. So that's one of the options we're giving you."

"You're sending me back to earth?"

"We're giving you a choice. Basically, we think you're dangerous but we haven't really got anything on you. So we don't want to lock you up here and waste our jail space either."

"It's a choice but I haven't got any other option?"

"Don't jump the gun. There is another option. We send you to either Clidurna or Blissaune. Your choice. We drop you at the border. You figure it out from there. Either way, we'll acquire your apartment and refund you the purchase price, and we'll let you move everything out. It's a pretty good deal we're offering you. You could be getting less."

"I'm getting kicked out all of a sudden, I'm not gonna have a place to live, and this is supposed to be a good deal? I've been here less than a week."

"Well, that's part of the reason why you're getting kicked out. We can't let you stay in Lintal, it's too dangerous to have someone suspicious like you around. So, your choice. Back to earth, off to Clidurna with your new-found friend Thurl, or will you reveal the truth why you're here and opt for Blissaune?"

"Haven't I got any time to think about it?"

"I'll give you five minutes. I'll leave the room. You'd better have an answer for me, or we won't even reimburse you the price of your apartment."

Chandor was shell-shocked by the suddenness of it all. His mind drew a blank. Nothing seemed to make sense. He tried to weigh the pros and cons of each option in his mind, and failed. All rational thought was lost.

The officer came back in.

"Well, so what'll we have?"

"I…"

"I'm giving you 5 seconds, and then you're gonna have nothing left."

"5"

"4"

"3"

"Clidurna it is. Contact Thurl for me."

"Well done. See, I knew a little pressure would do the trick. I'll call Thurl now."

The officer pressed his communicator. "Get me Thurl," he barked.

"Which Thurl do you want?"

"The one from Clidurna, stupid machine. He's the only Thurl we know from Clidurna."

"Please don't call me a stupid machine. Please wait."

In a few seconds, Thurl appeared in front of them.

"Hey, who's this? I don't think I know you," Thurl said, looking at the officer.

"Who I am doesn't matter. We are the Lintal police."

"Police? What's going on? I haven't done anything. My papers are all in order. Wait, isn't that Chandor?"

"Got that right, he's your friend Chandor. So, Chandor, why don't you tell Thurl what's going on?"

"Right. Thurl, I'm in a bit of a fix," said Chandor, "To cut the long story short, I'm getting kicked out of Lintal because the police find me suspicious, goodness knows why. I've opted to go to Clidurna."

"So you're taking up our job offer?"

"Yes."

"That's great!" Thurl beamed, then looked a bit embarrassed. "I mean, I'm sorry you're in whatever situation you're in, but I think this is for the better, no?"

"I guess…"

"So you guys had better work out the details of how you're gonna get picked up from the Clidurnian border and all that stuff. We'll send an officer to your apartment to watch you pack," interjected the officer, "How long do you need? Will an earth day be enough?"

"It should be enough, I've barely unpacked," replied Chandor.

"Right. So we're sending you back once we're done with Thurl here, then from there you'll have 24 hours to pack. So, Thurl, how are you going to pick our friend Chandor here up from the Clidurnian border?" asked the police officer.

"When will you arrive?"

"It's probably going to be about an hour by express capsule. It's now oh-9-hundred hours, earth Greenwich Mean Time, so let's say we get Chandor out of here within an hour, that's 10-hundred hours, then he's got 24 hours to pack, then it's another hour after that, so we'll probably be at the Clidurnian border by 11-hundred tomorrow. Can do?"

"Yes. I'll arrange for an express capsule on our end too, one that can fit all his belongings. I'll be waiting there from 10:30 onwards. Don't worry, Chandor, we'll arrange for a temporary place to stay for you in Clidurna until we can make some permanent arrangements."

"Right, so we're done here. Chandor, I wish you well. Don't come back to Lintal ever again," said the officer.

~

In no time, a police officer was escorting Chandor back to his apartment on an express capsule, moving through a special network of travellators.

"This is some secret path, eh?" asked Chandor.

"Don't ask so much. We're not supposed to tell you anything, you're under suspicion."

"Hey, lighten up, will you? Do I look like some kind of saboteur to you?"

"You know, they say real thieves never look like thieves. If you looked that suspicious, you'd get caught in a flash."

"Well, now you guys are already kicking me out of Lintal, so I must be an exceptional failure of a saboteur, if I even was one."

"Count your lucky stars you're getting out and not getting shot. This is the moon, you know. Not like earth. We can't afford to have all these human rights in a state of emergency."

"That's what all of you say. I hope Clidurna's better."

"I wouldn't bet my life on it," said the police officer, irate by now by Chandor's constant baiting. "Now, we're here. Shut up and go in and pack your stuff. You'll be transferred the refund on your apartment only after you're out of Lintal."

They arrived at the entrance of an elevator. "Unit B3-25," said the police officer, and the elevator whizzed to Chandor's apartment. In no time, they were right at Chandor's doorstep.

"Right. You go in, pack, and you're not allowed to come out or have contact with anyone until 24 hours later. I'll be right here making sure you don't come out."

"That's the new guy, isn't he?" Chandor heard the voice of one of the neighbours from the other day. He was standing a few doors away.

"Yeah, I knew something was up! Why else would the police be here?" remarked another neighbour.

"No talking to them, Chandor," reminded the officer, "Move along, now."

Chandor opened the door and went in. There was not very much to pack since, as he told the police, he had barely begun to unpack. He began stuffing all the items he could bring into his backpack.

The day's events had exhausted Chandor. Despite having slept the night before, once Chandor was done packing, he went to the bed, lay down, and soon fell into a deep sleep.

~

Chandor was awakened by the sound of his communicator.

"Who is it?" he asked sleepily.

"It's me, the police officer outside your door. It's about time. Wash up, grab your stuff and we'll be off."

"What about all the other stuff I can't bring? Like the furniture?"

"We'll compensate you for it. At cost price."

"Right, I guess that's the best I can hope for right now."

Chandor had a quick shower, brushed his teeth and grabbed his belongings, then headed out the door where the police officer was standing.

"Wow, where did you sleep last night? Were you standing there throughout?" he asked the police officer.

"None of your concern," the police officer answered brusquely.

They got on an elevator and got off outside an express capsule. They climbed into the express capsule and, within an hour, arrived in a large dome where many people were queueing. A sign above announced their destination: "Border Crossing from Lintal to Clidurna".

"Wow, looks like there's a long queue. How are we going to get to Thurl in time?" remarked Chandor.

"We get to skip the queue. Lucky you, huh?" The police officer led Chandor to a special gantry at the side. Chandor put his eyes to an iris scanner on the machine, before the machine said, "Recognised. Exit from Lintal permitted."

"Right. Off you go, then. Good luck," said the police officer.

Chandor walked through the gantry, then down a passageway. At the end of it, he scanned his eyes at another iris scanner. "Welcome to Clidurna," the scanner greeted him.

As Chandor walked through the gantry, he heard a voice call out.

"Chandor!"

It was Thurl.

IV.   A gargantuan task

"Boy, am I glad to see you," Chandor greeted Thurl. They began walking to a travellator and got into a capsule.

Thurl extended his hand and Chandor shook it. "Glad the deal we had for you was timely. What happened, really? Why'd they kick you out of Lintal all of a sudden?"

"It's ridiculous. There was a case of sabotage in my dome, you might have read about it in the news."

"Yes, I heard it was a job by Blissaune."

"So I got out of my apartment late at night to have a short walk outside. I wasn't able to sleep as I was thinking about your offer. To my surprise, I saw sirens and flashing lights everywhere. A neighbour told me it was sabotage by Blissaune.

A police officer came and asked me if there was anyone suspicious around recently. Then all of a sudden, 2 of my neighbours said I was suspicious as they hadn't seen me around

64

before. Just like that, the police decided to arrest me!

I didn't even know what was going on and they interrogated me and threw me into a lockup. Then I was told that I was suspicious because I had dealings with you, Kail & Nith after we just met, and you were from Clidurna. I don't even know how Clidurna figured into it when the suspected saboteurs were from Blissaune.

Next thing I knew, they told me they were kicking me out of Lintal and gave me a choice to either go back to earth or to go to Clidurna. I picked Clidurna, so here I am.

The police were just ridiculous. They kept saying that this is the moon, there are no human rights, security is paramount and so on."

"Yeah, that's the way it is," replied Thurl, sounding sympathetic, "Lintal is supposed to be somewhat democratic, but they don't really practice what they preach. I've even heard that they have the death penalty there, though that's, of course, something that they don't publicise a great deal. Barbarians behind a veneer of civility."

"Now, in Clidurna, we're different," he added proudly, "It's a dicey situation on the moon, but we try to respect everyone who comes here as best as we can. You made the right choice, Chandor. Everything worked out for good."

"Just a little unnerved by the suddenness of it all. Well, I guess at least you'll be setting me up here. Beats being completely lost."

"You have arrived," said the capsule as it opened. Chandor and Thurl stepped out of the capsule into a gleaming dome, full of shiny and sleek curved surfaces.

"Looks like I got an upgrade," remarked Chandor.

"Don't make too much of it. This is the town centre. We've got to take another travellator to the dome where you're new apartment is. We'll be working out the details with Lintal to transfer the refund from your apartment there and set it off against the purchase price of the apartment here. You'd like that, wouldn't you? Or would you prefer to rent?"

"I prefer having my own home, thanks. So I don't have to do anything? How does that work?"

"I'm a moon dust man. That's a big deal over here in Clidurna, so I've got some clout with our government. Leave the administrative stuff to us. We've got staff to do that. We want you to focus on your new job now that you've come here."

They walked to another travellator and got on it. In a few minutes, they were at another dome. This one had an old world charm, decorated in a Renaissance theme. Grooved columns were everywhere, as were sculptures and paintings.

"Wow, this is even nicer than the town centre!" remarked Chandor.

Thurl laughed. "You know what they say, we're kind of like Europe on earth and Lintal is like the United States, based on the system of governance. So we like having a bit of a classical European theme here, too. Except that while America is perceived to be more technologically advanced than Europe on earth, we're the more technologically advanced nation on the moon," Thurl said proudly.

They got into an elevator and arrived outside Chandor's door. "Right, so have a rest, you need it after such an upheaval. We'll meet tomorrow morning and I'll brief you on what happens next. Your apartment's fully furnished. I assume you've got all you need and you don't need anything more from your erstwhile apartment in Lintal?"

"I think I'm fine, this is all I brought."

"Good. See you tomorrow morning, Chandor. I'll be right here."

Thurl went back into the elevator and left.

Chandor opened the door. Like the rest of the dome, his apartment, too, was decorated in a classical Greek / Italian style. The door opened into a small corridor decorated with fake pillars on both sides. The corridor led into a hall with a large faux-marble dining table in the centre. Beside that was the kitchen, with a countertop that looked like it was granite. Chandor knocked on it, wondering if it was really granite. It felt and sounded like some kind of very hard plastic instead.

Maybe it's made of moon dust, Chandor thought.

Chandor went into the only bedroom. It was a cozy little nest, with an imitation fireplace at the wall. The bed looked luxurious too, with ornate carvings on its frame. All in all, it looked a lot better than the apartment back in Lintal.

Wow, they're pulling out all the stops for me. I guess I'll be paying for this, but why are they even doing this for me? Chandor wondered. *I wonder what's the catch.*

Chandor headed to the bathroom, which was exquisite like the rest of the apartment, with a black and white checkerboard pattern for the floor, with shiny ivory finishings all over.

Well, never mind worrying about what's the catch for now. I gotta take a bath and get some rest.

Chandor had a shower and headed to bed, where he quickly fell into a deep sleep, tired out by the rapid changes that had taken place in the past few days.

~

"You have a visitor."

Chandor woke with a start. He got up and headed to the hall, where he saw a holographic image of Thurl standing inside the door. Thurl was looking around, seeming to be unable to see him.

I guess only I can see visitors from inside, but they can't see what's in the apartment from outside. Handy, he thought.

"Open the door," he commanded.

The old-style door, made of imitation wood and with real hinges, like a door on earth, opened to reveal Thurl in the flesh.

"Morning! Just got up, I see," Thurl greeted Chandor, who was still in his pyjamas, "I think you need some time to wash up and get some breakfast. We stocked the larder with food, by the way. Although it's foam. But it's nutritious and doesn't taste that bad."

"Come on in and have a seat," Chandor replied. Thurl stepped into the room and sat down on a plush sofa at the side of the hall, with curved handles and also made of imitation wood.

Chandor headed to the bathroom to wash, brush his teeth and change. After he came out and headed for the larder, grabbed a packet, and hydrated it with a water gun.

"For mush, it doesn't taste all that bad," he remarked to Thurl. Interestingly enough, it was actually pretty tasty. Chandor turned the packet to look at the label. It read "Chicken Mushroom Mashed Potato".

"Which one did you get?" asked Thurl.

"Chicken Mushroom Mashed Potato," replied Chandor.

"Not a bad choice. The taste is there, it's just the mouthfeel that's a bit lacking."

Chandor finished his breakfast and before Thurl and he headed out to the travelators.

"So, what happens today?" asked Chandor as the capsule which they got in sped along.

"Today, you're going to meet the big boss. He meets every new hire. He'll let you know exactly what you're going to be working on. Secret stuff, but not top secret - we don't give top secret information to new employees. Then I'll bring you back to the town centre and we'll have a short tour. How do you find your apartment?"

"Very posh, much more plush than in Lintal. Is it expensive? I guess I'll have to pay for it."

"Don't worry, basically, we'll set off the refund from your Lintal apartment against the price of this place, and the company will top up the balance. It doesn't cost all that much, anyway. Classical architecture is the default style in Clidurna. There are plenty of interior designers who do this, so it comes relatively cheap."

"The company will top up the balance? Seriously, why are you guys being so nice to me? I haven't even started work yet."

"Haha, you don't know what you've gotten yourself into," Thurl gave a somewhat ominous laugh. Seeing the alarm on Chandor's face, Thurl added, "Just kidding, don't worry. You probably took it a bit seriously given what you've been through in the past week. We do this for most of our professional new hires. Perks of the job. You impressed me with your chemical engineering experience and we need a chemical engineer urgently, so there's no way we're going to shortchange you."

The capsule came to a halt. "Here we are," said Thurl, getting out of the capsule. Chandor climbed out, to be greeted by the sight of another shiny dome, in the same style as the town centre. A holographic image in the centre of the dome said "Lunasilico".

"That's us." Thurl pointed to the sign. "Lunasilico. You should know what that means. We're not a corporation. We're not strictly a government department either. We're something in between, kind of like what you'd call a research institute on earth. Don't get me going on the legalities of it, it's going to bore you. Over here. We're going to head to the big boss' office."

Thurl and Chandor entered an elevator, gleaming and sleek just like the rest of the dome. "The ufo," Thurl commanded.

"The ufo?" Chandor looked puzzled.

"Comes from an earth term, UFO, unidentified flying object, I'm sure you know. It's just that we pronounce it as a word here. We call the big boss' office that because it's a sort of circular disk that sticks out of the top of the dome, so it looks like a flying saucer, earth's typical rendition of what a UFO usually looks like."

The doors opened. As Chandor stepped out, he saw that the elevator's arrival pod was right in the middle of the office. As was the case for the Lunsilico dome, everything was shiny, either metallic or white.

"Welcome!" a slim elderly woman, with frizzled grey hair, sitting behind a desk in front of him called out. "You must be Chandor. We have been expecting you."

"Our big boss, Chandor," Thurl added.

"Please, call me Svielyar," the woman said, extending her hand. Chandor walked up to the desk and shook Svielyar's hand. "How has Clidurna been treating you so far?"

"I've just arrived, but it's certainly been better than my horrid experience in Lintal. I'm sure you've heard about it already."

"Yes, I have. What a way to treat a person." Svielyar sounded sympathetic, "Have a seat. I gather you're a chemical engineer and Thurl has told me about your experiences on earth. Good job you did there with the toxic waste. Tell me, what do you know about moon dust?"

"I haven't had the chance to work with it," said Chandor, somewhat bashfully, "But I know that it's mostly silica. Hence your organisation's name. And I know that it's a nuisance to most people, but it's really important to Clidurna."

"Yes, you're right. Everybody thinks of it as dust and treats it like a waste material, but it's really valuable when you know what to do with it. Look at these walls. What do you think they're made of?"

"Moon dust?"

"Exactly. Look at the furnishings in your house. Look at all the realistic imitation wood we have. What do you think they're made of?"

"Wow, I never guessed that even the imitation wood was made of moon dust. It was very true to life."

"See? Moon dust is gold. In fact, better than gold. There's so much that we do with it in Clidurna. That's why we're richer than Lintal and Blissaune. They know we're into moon dust, but they don't know the extent to which our economy is dependent on it. That's why we export loads of moon dust products to earth, but nobody knows we do. We're quiet about it. The situation on the moon is too dicey to let Lintal and Blissaune find out the secret of our wealth."

"Sounds amazing. From what I've read on earth, the early astronauts found moon dust to be both a mechanical problem and a health hazard. It gummed up the space suits and inhaling it would give you silicosis."

"That's right. Moon dust is amazing, but it's also dangerous. Very dangerous. That's part of the reason why Lintal and Blissaune don't touch it. Moon dust is fatal, to both machines and humans. But we've got the technology to prevent it. But we've hit a limiting factor."

"What's that?"

"This is where you fit in, Chandor. Our moon dust harvesters are working, but they are not working all that well. And we've got some of our staff, who operate the harvesters directly, becoming ill. Now, you know that in Clidurna, we do actually have rights. So they could very well take legal action against us if they can prove that they're illness was due to moon dust, which they're exposed to in the course of their work. That would pose a real problem to us because we're not your run-of-the-mill limited liability corporation. We're government-linked. A scandal could bring down the whole of Clidurna. That's why when we found out about your experience on earth, we thought it would come in handy."

"And my job is to…"

"Come up with something that can neutralise the toxic effects of moon dust and it's tendency to gum up machines. Something that can be easily deployed in our harvesters. Maybe something that can coagulate the moon dust into blocks so it can't get breathed in or can't get into gaps, I don't know. It's best if you can develop one solution that solves both problems, but the health issue is a priority. Once you've managed to find something, we'll get our doctors to find a safe way to test it out on animals, then perhaps it can be made into a cure for our sick employees. It would be even better if you could make something like that out of moon dust itself."

Chandor whistled. "Sounds like a tall order. You're essentially asking for a magic pill."

"We are, Chandor. And we're betting on you. Even though we barely know you. But any chemical engineer is worth a shot. Most of our own people have turned us away. The responsibility is too great, they think, and they lack the confidence."

"I see. So, when do I start?"

"You start work on Monday. It's Saturday now, in case you've forgotten - it's a little hard to keep track of time on the moon. So you've got tomorrow to rest and mull over the problem, then on Monday, you head to the lab. We'll need you to really put your nose to the grindstone on this one."

"Right. I'll try my best."

"You either do it or you don't do it. There is no 'try'. Lives are depending on you. You're not the only one we've hired for this, of course, we've got a team, but it's good if you felt personally responsible for this project."

"What happens if I fail?"

"Well, let's just say that you're here in Clidurna on an employment pass which we applied for, so you're permitted to be here as long as you work for us. If we find that you can't do the work that we've assigned to you, your employment comes to an end and so does your employment pass."

"I thought we had rights in Clidurna."

"For sure. You'll be given hearings before the employment pass is terminated, opportunities to find other employment in Clidurna so you don't have to leave, that's if you want to stay of course, and so on. But we're the biggest employer of chemical engineers. If we don't want you, the likelihood is that you're going to have to leave Clidurna. You're not Clidurnian, at least not yet, so we don't need to keep you here. It's as simple as that."

"Now, let's not scare Chandor out of his wits when he's just come," Thurl interjected with a smile. "Svielyar, why don't I show him around, then bring him to the town centre?"

"Sure thing. Now, Chandor, you'll be reporting to Thurl, but I will keep track of your progress personally as well and I'll speak to you from time to time. All the best, and I do hope you'll be able to find us our magic pill." Svielyar arose to shake Chandor's hand, then Thurl led

Chandor back to the elevator and out of the office.

V.　　Race against time

"So, how do you find Svielyar?" asked Thurl.

"A bit intimidating, to be honest. This job doesn't look like it's going to be an easy one," replied Chandor.

"Right, it definitely isn't and that's why we're putting as many brains as we can on this right now. I've been growing my team for several months now. They're all off work today, but I'll introduce you to the rest of the team on Monday. But first, let's show you around Clidurna!"

Chandor and Thurl hopped onto a travelator. "Why aren't we taking a capsule?" Chandor asked.

"This takes slightly longer, but you can see more when you're not in a capsule. See, over here's our spaceport." Thurl pointed to a bustling area where people and containers of goods moved around at rapid pace. Through the glass roof of the spaceport, Chandor could see rockets rapidly blasting off.

"Looks a lot busier than Lintal."

"You bet, we do a lot of business with earth."

"Let me guess, moon dust?"

Thurl laughed. "We told you that already."

As they changed travellators, they passed through a noisy thoroughfare where loud music was playing.

"Pubs? I guess this is the downtown area?"

"Yes, a little bit of earth's culture that we've brought over. Clidurna's put them all in one place to give it a bohemian feel. A little different from Lintal where your typical watering hole is nondescript and mixed among apartment units."

After passing through a few other domes which seemed to comprise predominantly of apartments and offices, they arrived at the town centre.

"There. We're a little different from Lintal here. While we've got shops mixed among apartments as well, we actually have a town centre in each neighbourhood. This town's known as Vite."

"What does that mean?" asked Chandor.

"Vite is the French word for fast and is pronounced 'vit'," Thurl explained, "It's meant to convey the meaning of the fast, lively pace of this town. The elevator network has a mesh system, which means that there's an almost direct link between any 2 points so travelling between any 2 units in the town centre is super fast."

"I'm starting to not get surprised about how advanced Clidurna is," remarked Chandor

"Getting used to it, huh? So let's show you around the neighbourhood."

They got into an elevator. "The cleaning robot shop," said Thurl.

"What, the most exciting thing here is supposed to be cleaning robots?" asked Chandor in disbelief.

"Hey, it might be boring but you don't want to be scrambling around to find it when your cleaning robot stops working," replied Thurl, "Besides, you haven't seen our cleaning robots."

They arrived at the door of the cleaning robot shop. "Welcome!" a cleaning robot at the door greeted them. "Can I show you around?"

"Cleaning robots show people around? I thought for the most part they just ran in the background and vacuumed stuff, or whatever," remarked Chandor.

"Yes, it's a little different from earth or even Lintal where cleaning robots are mere machines that move around quietly and clean things. You can set your cleaning robot to that mode here in Clidurna, but that's a waste. We like to make our robots here personable. Yes, show us around," Thurl addressed the robot.

"Right this way, gentlemen." The robot brought them to a dazzling array of various cleaning robots of all shapes, sizes and colours.

"Looks like you folks are an artistic lot here. Most of the cleaning robots on earth look like cylinders or boxes, in grey or beige. Here they're colourful sculptures and most of them have some sort of face or head," remarked Chandor.

"Yup. But anyway, you've already got a cleaning robot in your apartment, and you won't be needing to buy a new one soon. Show us to the repair area," Thurl addressed the robot again.

"Follow me," said the robot. It stopped outside a large hole in the wall which had a holographic image hovering in front of it which looked like a spanner.

"So, Chandor. If you ever need any servicing done, just drop off your cleaning robot into that hole in the wall and it'll be shipped off to the servicing machines. It'll be done in less than a day and your communicator will prompt you when it's time to collect it again."

"Got that. A useful thing to know," said Chandor.

For the rest of the day, Nith brought Chandor around the town centre, showing him all manner of shops selling apparel, equipment, and even tourist souvenirs. Then they rounded off the day in a restaurant in Chandor's dome named "Greek & Italian Classico".

"Something unique to this dome, huh? I guess that's why we didn't eat in the town centre," remarked Chandor.

"Oh, more than that, this is one of the top ten must-try restaurants in the Lunasilico guide! That's like the Michelin guide on earth," Thurl nodded enthusiastically.

"Wait, isn't Lunasilico who we work for?"

"Yes. Just like how Michelin is a tyre manufacturer on earth but it produces a food guide, so it is with Lunasilico. We have so many people working for us, always swapping tips on where to find the best chow, that we started publishing a food guide. So now that's what we're best known for, apart from moon dust. Perhaps it's even better known than the moon dust operations since much of the moon dust ops are so hush-hush."

"Amazing. They say you learn a new thing every day, but I'm learning heaps of new things just in one day," replied Chandor.

Thurl raised his glass. "Cheers, to working together!"

"Cheers! You're so nice out of work, I hope you're nice as a boss too."

"Don't worry, I'm the nicest boss you could find in Lunasilico. The rest of them are much too serious. That said, I expect good work to be done, but that usually isn't a problem because I've been pretty good at spotting good engineers so far. My gut told me that you're a good chemical engineer, even though you haven't started work for us yet."

They clinked their glasses together.

~

Sunday whizzed by, and before Chandor knew it, Monday was here. Chandor woke up and washed up, then headed to Lunasilico for his first day at work.

"Chandor!" greeted Thurl once Chandor was at the office. "Let me introduce you to the rest of the company."

Thurl brought Chandor round several departments, introducing them to the important people there. Finally, they arrived back at their own office.

"So, finally, our own team. This is Kaylor, also a chemical engineer like you, specialising in organic chemistry."

Kaylor, a petite black woman, came and shook Chandor's hand. "Welcome to Clidurna, I hear you're from out of town."

"Yes, I am."

"And this is Hadille, our lab technician. Very important chap."

Chandor shook Hadille's hand. Hadille was a stout, burly caucasian man. "I hear you're an expert," Hadille said.

"Is that what Thurl has been telling you guys?"

"Well, I might have told the rest a thing or 2 about you. Might," Thurl shrugged his shoulders. "And this is Midah, also a chemical engineer, specialising in volatile compounds."

"Good to have another hand on deck, Chandor," said Midah, an asian man like Chandor.

"So, that's all of the team. We're a small team, Chandor. So now that you know the team, I'm going to bring you around to see the machines. We've got some powerful stuff."

Thurl led Chandor to a very cold room. "This is our supercomputer. We call her Crunchie since she crunches numbers so fast. 200 exaflops. She can simulate just about any molecule you want and she predicts chemical reactions with a frightening accuracy, even for as-yet-unknown substances."

"Sounds impressive, and faster than anything I've seen on earth. So we just connect to her with our communicators to use her?"

"Yes, she uses all the standard protocols. Just use her like she's an extension of your communicator. That said, she's popular, and everybody's scrambling to use her all the time, so everyone's usage is time-limited. Not a problem most of the time, though, since she's so fast, and you can always borrow time from one of our teammates if you want."

Thurl brought Chandor to another room with a criss-crossed network of tubes and test-tubes. "This is the chemistry lab. You can mix loads of chemicals in here. There's options for you to control the temperature, pressure and just about everything else you can think of. The chemicals are mixed for you when you press a button. There's a small area over there where you can do manual work as well."

They left the chemistry lab for a room full of robotic vehicles. "Here's the harvester bay. These are the harvesters we use to harvest moon dust. They're all specially treated to make sure the moon dust doesn't gum them up, but of course, as you already know, they're far from perfect. That's something you'll be working on as well. This the first time you're seeing a moon dust harvester?"

"Yes. Well, it looks like what I expected. Tracked propulsion, lots of mechanical parts," replied Chandor.

Thurl brought Chandor to a several other rooms to show him various other pieces of equipment. By the time they were done seeing everything, the work day had ended.

"Have a good rest, Chandor. It's your first day, so I recommend that you go home for now. There's plenty of opportunity for you to work overtime once work gets in full swing" Thurl chuckled.

Chandor headed home, his head still spinning from the array of different things he had seen. It would take him a while to get familiar with everything he was shown.

~

The next few days were hectic for Chandor as he was plunged into a frenetic pace of work. While Thurl was a genial boss, he was nevertheless demanding and never ceased to emphasise that progress must be made, and quickly. The rest of the team was keenly aware of the pressure that they were facing to develop what Lunasilico needed to address the crisis, and fast, and their energy was infectious.

It was after several weeks that Chandor first began to notice something strange in some of the reagents he had been testing with moon dust.

"Hey Thurl, look at this." Chandor and Thurl were in the lab.

"What gives?"

"That's something I haven't seen before."

"What are you using on the moon dust?"

"I ran gas chromatography mass spectrometry on the moon dust. Then I separated out this substance, which I sent to the particle accelerator. I bombarded it with darmstadtium atoms."

"Then what happened?"

"Look at this rat." Chandor had been testing his new compound on a live rat which had been exposed to moon dust.

The rat's skin, visible under its fur, had turned almost completely blue in colour. The rat was breathing heavily and rapidly and looked like it was about to die.

"Oh my," remarked Thurl. "That doesn't look like a cure."

"Quite the opposite, in fact. It seems like I've created a compound that accelerates the effects of silicosis, making it almost immediate. As you know, cyanosis, or skin turning blue, is one of the effects of silicosis. My compound has turned this rat blue all over almost instantaneously."

"Well, this isn't what we're looking for, but I think it's a hazard we must take note of. There's lots of darmstadtium on the moon, and there could well be even more serious illnesses on our hands. Those working directly with moon dust, even ourselves, are at tremendous risk. I will need to speak to Svielyar about this. I'll arrange a meeting together with Svielyar as well as the rest of the team, and I'll need you around, Chandor."

~

The day of the meeting came. Chandor, Thurl and the rest of their team were in Svielyar's office.

"Why don't you begin, Chandor?" asked Thurl.

"Well, I was working on finding the antidote to moon dust. So I had done a gas chromatography mass spectrometry on the moon dust. I separated out a substance which I bombarded with Darmstadtium atoms in the particle accelerator. Then I tested it on a rat which had gotten silicosis from previous exposure to moon dust."

"That rat has since died, so I've brought another of the rats in the lab here." Chandor held up the small enclosure, transparent all around, which he brought.

Chandor touched a blinking light on the enclosure and a powdery substance dropped from a small canister on the roof of the enclosure to the floor of the enclosure. Everyone could see the powdery substance visibly get inhaled by the rat.

"Ghn! Ghn!" Everyone could see the rat coughing and breathing hard. Gradually, the skin of the rat, partially visible under its fur, began to turn blue.

Within a few minutes, the rat was dead.

"I know this isn't what we've set out to find. I haven't found a cure yet, but I think I've found the opposite. I've found that bombarding this compound within moon dust with Darmstadtium dramatically accelerates the rate of death from silicosis. There's lots of Darmstadtium on the moon. We've got to review all our mining operations to ensure that nobody is exposed to a similar chemical if it occurs naturally."

"This is quite a serious issue for Clidurna's security. Our enemies could very well find out about this and contaminate our moon dust supplies with Darmstadtium to accelerate the onset of silicosis in our mining staff. It would be a disaster if that happened, and I wouldn't put it past Blissaune to pull off a stunt like that, if they knew how to," mused Svielyar.

"What do you think we should do about this?" asked Midah.

"There are national security implications," Kaylor chimed in. "Do we have to escalate this to the political leaders?"

"Yes, I think I'll have to speak to the Chancellor so we can take some action to safeguard Clidurna against this. You must all keep this top secret, of course. I'd say good work, Chandor - but not quite, not yet: now that you've found another hazard for us, what we need is yet another antidote for this." Svielyar looked at Chandor.

"Right. Unfortunately, this wasn't the discovery we were hoping for but I guess this is how science is. Sometimes you don't find what you were looking for and you find something else instead. Sometimes it's helpful, like penicillin. And sometimes, like now, we discover something more dangerous," replied Chandor.

"Well, let Svielyar speak to the Chancellor and then we'll decide what we have to do next. Until then, continue working on what you're currently working on," Thurl added. With that, the team left the meeting.

~

Several days passed, with little progress made by the team in any direction, before Thurl summoned the team's members again.

"Svielyar's spoken to the Chancellor. He wants to know just how dangerous this new compound is. He wants a demonstration, so Chandor, I guess you have to publicly sacrifice another rat."

"When does he want to see us?" asked Hadille.

"Actually, he wants to see us today," replied Thurl.

"Talk about short notice," said Chandor.

"Well, you don't exactly have to do a lot to prepare, do you?" Thurl responded.

"Just have to do another bombardment with Darmstadtium atoms again. It'll be done in a jiffy," replied Chandor.

"Then get to work pronto, we're seeing him in a couple of hours. So, the rest of you guys, gather here in 2 hours and be ready to see the

Chancellor. In the meanwhile, Chandor, get cracking."

Chandor went back to the lab and prepared another rat in a transparent enclosure, then went about preparing the necessary chemicals for the demonstration.

In about 2 hours, Chandor was done.

"Right. Shall we get going?" asked Thurl.

"Ready when you are," replied Chandor.

The team set off along a network of travelators, then finally got into a special armoured receptacle which looked like a cross between a travelator capsule and an elevator.

"Wow, security is tight," remarked Chandor as the capsule closed.

"What do you expect, it's the Chancellor's office. It's not like we get to see him everyday," said Thurl.

The capsule sped along, and in no time at all, they popped up right in the middle of a large, but spartan, office. The office was empty except for a desk and a man sitting behind it.

"Good to see you again, Thurl. How long has it been since we last met?" asked the man as the capsule opened.

"I think it's been a few years," answered Thurl. "And, as always, there's a new crisis to deal with. Chandor, this is our Chancellor, Crull."

"Ah, so this is Chandor," the Chancellor remarked drily. "We asked you to find a cure, and instead you found us a poison."

"Most unfortunate, sir," Chandor responded.

"Now, you don't have to call me sir. As Thurl has said, I'm Crull."

"And this is the rest of the team, Crull," Thurl interjected, "Kaylor, Hadille and Midah."

"Pleased to meet all of you. I'm sure all of you Clidurnians know who I am, so I won't bother with a self-introduction. So, Chandor. You have a demonstration for us."

"Yes, I do." Chandor produced the transparent enclosure. The rat was running around in the transparent enclosure.

Chandor touched the blinking light on the enclosure and, just like in the demonstration in Svielyar's office, a powdery substance dropped from a small canister on the roof of the enclosure to the floor of the enclosure. Again, everyone could see the powdery substance get inhaled by the rat.

"Ghn! Ghn!" As everyone, save for Crull, had seen before, the rat coughed and breathed hard. Gradually, the skin of the rat, partially visible under its fur, began to turn blue.

Splat! One of the blood vessels on the rat's head burst, spurting a shower of blood on the transparent walls of the enclosure.

"Good grief!" exclaimed Crull.

"Wow, I didn't expect that myself," remarked Chandor.

"Ugh. This looks scarier than the last time," Svielyar added.

"Certainly a dangerous substance, and one that we need to safeguard against our enemies getting their hands on. Blissaune would love to get their hands on something like this, given their penchant for sabotage and murder. The question is, what do we do now that we've found out about this substance but we haven't found a cure yet?" Crull asked.

There was an awkward silence as nobody knew what answer to give.

"Well, I suppose that's my job," Crull broke the silence. "That's what you good Clidurnians elected me for. You guys are just supposed to develop the chemicals and all that. So, Chandor." He looked at Chandor. "I guess we'll have to meet up a few more times from now on to discuss this."

"Certainly," answered Chandor.

"Well, it was good seeing all of you today, even though the literally bloody demonstration wasn't exactly a pleasant show. Thank you for coming along with Chandor, everyone. I'll think about what we can do to safeguard Clidurna's security, and I'll be meeting with Chandor alone from now on so the rest of you won't have to come along."

"A pleasure to meet you, Crull," said Kaylor. Thurl and the team got back into the capsule and left Crull's office.

VI.   Enemy or friend?

"Guess we've added more problems to his plate, haven't we?" Chandor asked Thurl rhetorically as they sat in the capsule.

"Nothing Clidurna can't deal with. If anything, the strength of Clidurna lies in the fact that decisions aren't Crull's job to make alone. So that's how we differ from despotic states like Blissaune. Even Lintal, a supposed democracy, falls short - over there, too much power is concentrated in one man, the president. Here we pride ourselves on collective decision making," replied Thurl.

After some small talk between Chandor, Thurl and the rest of the team, silence set in as all of them began to think about the implications of what Chandor had just discovered and how they could go about finding a remedy.

They soon arrived back at the headquarters of Lunasilico. The day passed slowly for Chandor, as he was stumped and could make no progress. He occupied himself with busywork, waiting for the day to pass until he could get home.

The next day, Chandor was back in the office when he received a call on his communicator. Oddly enough, the call was voice only and the other party had disabled the usual holographic video capabilities.

"Who is it?" Chandor asked the communicator.

"Unidentified," it replied, adding to the mystery.

Chandor debated in his mind whether to pick up the call. It was rare for callers not to identify themselves, at least on earth. *Perhaps this is moon culture*, he thought, *I don't know enough yet*. In the end, he decided to answer the call.

"Chandor!" a somewhat familiar, yet unfamiliar, voice called out.

"Is that Chancellor Crull?" Chandor guessed.

"Yes. And Crull will be fine. So, I told you yesterday that we would be talking more about that discovery of yours."

"Yes, I presume you called me to talk about it?"

"Of course. But not over the phone. That's earth-speak for a communicator, isn't it? Now, you may be wondering why I'm not appearing holographically and why I didn't identify myself when calling. I don't want your colleagues to know about this. I want to keep our discussions as hush hush as possible. I'm sure you appreciate the gravity of the situation."

"Yes, of course, sir - I mean, Crull."

"Good. Now, I would like you to meet with me again, as well as with 2 other legislators, to brief us on the situation. We don't want any of your colleagues coming along, not even Thurl, so don't breathe a word to any of them. When can you make it?"

"Whenever it's suitable for you, Crull." Chandor deferred to the Chancellor on this.

"Well, the sooner the better, then. Come over after lunch. Tell Thurl you have something personal to attend to, then head over to my office. You remember the way?"

"Not really."

"Don't worry. Just say this code to the express capsule once you get in and it'll automagically find it's way to my office. The elevator shaft in my office is not a normal one. Express travellator capsules can go in it too." Crull gave Chandor the code.

After lunch, Chandor told Thurl that he needed to attend to a personal matter. Thurl frowned, but did not probe and told Chandor he could go off for the day. Chandor headed off to the travellators and said the code to the capsule, and off he went, hurtling through the travellators and into the elevator shaft, before popping up in the middle of Crull's office again.

"Chandor, welcome! It's good to see you here again, and I'm glad you're on time," Crull greeted him. "Meet my 2 colleagues, Representatives Bink," he gestured to his left, "and Clobb," he motioned to his right.

Bink was a woman with a short, wiry frame, who looked part asian and part caucasian. She looked somewhat older than Crull, and reminded Chandor a little of Svielyar. She wore spectacles, a strange choice of fashion since myopia had been curable at birth since a long time ago.

"Wondering about the spectacles?" She gave a short, tinkly laugh, reading Chandor's mind. "They're fake, of course. I enjoy watching historical dramas about earth. It's a fashion statement. Way back when, spectacles made one look respectable."

Clobb was a man of average build, with an olive complexion and slightly afro hair. He looked otherwise unremarkable, with a face that looked like it could fit in anywhere.

"Pleased to meet you, Chandor," he greeted Chandor as well.

"Now, lady and gents, I'm sure you know why we're here," said Crull. "Lunasilico hired Chandor to find a cure for silicosis, and instead, he discovered a more potent, deadly, accelerated way to induce silicosis. Let's just take a look at what Chandor showed us yesterday. I don't think another live demonstration is necessary, and Chandor didn't bring the equipment anyway. Chandor, this is the first time they're seeing this."

A holographic video began to play in front of them. It appeared that Crull had cut out most of the video except the crucial part. The video showed Chandor pressing the button, then the rat turning blue, and finally it's blood vessel bursting and spraying blood all over the enclosure.

Bink and Clobb both gasped.

"A dangerous substance indeed," said Bink.

"Not for the faint hearted. Now, I think we need to start manufacturing this stuff in bulk." At this, Chandor looked quizzically at Crull. "So we can do more experiments and hopefully find a cure," Crull added.

"Is it even safe to handle this?" asked Clobb.

"Well, Chandor managed to put it in an enclosure," answered Crull. "Chandor, how did you do it?"

"There wasn't much to it. You've got lots of robots. I could easily build a canister to dispense the chemical with the right programming. Of course, I didn't even have to handle the stuff directly myself. If I did, I'd have ended up like that rat in the video," Chandor replied.

"So it's a dangerous, fatal chemical, yet capable of being handled safely. Interesting," mused Clobb.

"And easily dispensed by a canister." Bink nodded thoughtfully.

"Yes, of course, so we need to find a cure for this," Crull added.

Seemed a bit hasty to jump in, thought Chandor. *I wonder what's afoot?*

"I know we're quite far from being able to find a cure, so what we really do need is an ability to make more of this stuff for testing so we can accelerate the process. Probably see if we can develop a way to produce it in canisters quickly," Crull said to Chandor.

"Why do we need to do that? I mean, it's enough that we can make small batches, that's good enough for testing purposes. And this chemical is dangerous. We don't want it falling into the wrong hands." Chandor was puzzled.

"Now, Chandor. You're a man of science. And science is nothing if not for empirical methods. We can't be running to you all the time to cook up a batch of this chemical. We want it accessible to all the scientists in your department on demand. And that means it has to be quickly produced, stored safely in canisters, ready for use when needed so that you guys can test out as many antidotes as possible," Crull replied.

A slick and smooth response, thought Chandor. *I wonder if there's something wrong here.*

"Now, folks," Crull continued, "I think Chandor here is on to something, and this clearly has national security implications. The 2 of you are on the parliamentary national security committee. Chandor, Lunasilico may be your employer - but as you know, the Clidurnian government does have some degree of oversight over Lunasilico. I propose that we entrust Chandor with the task of developing a system to mass produce canisters of this new and deadly chemical, for the purposes of experimentation, and his other duties will take a back seat for the time being. What say you?"

"Wait a minute, don't I get a say in this?" Chandor interrupted.

"Well, I guess you do - but you're not a Clidurnian yet. You're here on a work visa, so, you know, if you don't want to work for Lunasilico anymore..." Crull shrugged his shoulders.

"I thought this place was supposed to be more democratic than Lintal," Chandor retorted.

"Well, it is - but this is urgent stuff, Chandor. You're doing this so we can make more progress in our research to find a cure. And I'm the Chancellor of Clidurna. Why would I ask you to do anything unless it's for the good of Clidurna?" Crull's voice was suspiciously smooth.

"It is a good idea, Crull," Bink chimed in. "Chandor. What's the matter with you? We're asking you to produce this for research purposes. There's nothing unethical about it. Why are you so uptight?"

Chandor could not put his finger on it, but things did not feel quite right. Still, what Bink said made some sense - why was he refusing to do something which was simply in the course of his work?

"I concur, Bink," Clobb added, "This will help the work of the rest of his team members in Lunasilico. It's no loss at all to take him off his usual duties to focus on producing this chemical. Chandor, think about it - the more of this you produce, the faster the rest will find a cure."

With everybody putting pressure on him, Chandor felt trapped.

"I...I can't think of any reason why I shouldn't do this," Chandor muttered.

"Very wise of you, Chandor." Crull smiled warmly. "Don't worry, it'll all be done during your work hours anyway. We'll tell Thurl you're working on something related to your discovery. But we're not going to tell him exactly what you're doing. Producing this chemical is deadly and dangerous. If word leaks out and the chemical finds itself in the wrong hands, it'll be disastrous. So I don't want you to talk to even Thurl or the rest of your team about what you're doing exactly. Complete radio silence. Got that?"

Chandor was puzzled as to why there was such a great need for secrecy when the rest of his team already knew about his discovery. If the purpose of producing the canisters was to find a cure, and if they were supposed to use what he produced for their own work anyway, why could he not let them know what he was doing? But something about Crull's manner made him feel that it was not a good idea to vocalise his thoughts aloud.

"You have my word, Crull," he answered finally.

"Good. I want daily updates from you on your progress from now on. You'll report to the 3 of us directly. Now, you can go back to the office and get cracking. I'm sure you'll have good news for us soon."

Chandor left Crull's office and returned to Lunasilico. He wondered why Crull's instructions seemed so sinister. He could not understand the need to mass produce the deadly concoction for research purposes, but then again, wasn't most empirical research done by experimentation? They would need more of this chemical to produce a cure. But something about all of it did not make sense to him.

He returned to the office with a heavy heart. Once he arrived, Thurl beckoned to him.

"Just got off the communicator with Crull, Chandor. He says you're being put on a special project related to your discovery, and it's so top secret that even I can't know what exactly it's about. So, it seems like you're a VIP now, Chandor," Thurl joked.

"Yeah, not exactly my choice," Chandor responded softly, "Is this common?"

"Well, it's certainly not common, but then again, neither was your discovery. I've heard of this happening before, though - some of our staff reporting directly to the Chancellor on special projects from time to time. Don't worry, I'm totally cool with not knowing anything about what you're doing," Thurl reassured Chandor.

Thurl's reassurance put Chandor somewhat at ease.

Chandor spent the rest of the day in the lab, trying to find a way to speed up the bombardment of the moon dust with Darmstadtium. The next few weeks passed in similar fashion, with Chandor trying out various methods to speed up the process.

Eventually, Chandor managed to develop a method that would produce about 10 canisters of Darmstadtium bombarded moon dust a day. While that could hardly be said to be mass production, it was at least a start and it was progress that he could report to Crull.

Finally, once Chandor was ready, he called Crull on his communicator.

Crull picked up the call. "Ah, Chandor. Good news, I hope."

"Well, it's kind of good news. I've managed to develop a system to produce about 10 canisters a day. That should be enough for research purposes."

"Not bad, not bad at all. How about you come to my office and discuss this?"

"Sure, when?"

"How about now? I've got a slot free for you."

"Right, I'll head over." Chandor ended the call and headed out to the travelators to ride the capsule to Crull's office.

As the elevator doors opened in Crull's office, Chandor saw Crull speaking with Bink and Clobb. Crull did not notice that the elevator had arrived in his office and continued talking to Bink and Clobb, facing away from Chandor.

"So, like I was saying, this new canister will really come in useful. There are a few members of the opposition who are real pests. I'm sure you know who we're talking about."

The conversation did not seem quite right to Chandor, and he tried to listen intently without moving. Unfortunately, at that moment, Bink noticed him.

"Crull. Chandor's here." Bink pointed to Chandor.

Crull swiveled around, appearing somewhat startled.

"Oh hello, Chandor. Great to have you here, as always."

"The pleasure is mine," Chandor replied hollowly, feeling that something decidedly fishy was going on.

"So, Chandor, as you can see I have Representatives Bink and Clobb here with me again. We're very excited to hear about your progress."

Chandor wondered at that moment whether he should refrain from sharing his progress. However, it would be futile as he had already told Crull that he had developed a method to produce about 10 canisters a day.

"Well, as I told Crull, I've developed a method to produce about 10 canisters a day. It's not a lot, but I think that would be sufficient for our research purposes. So I think I'll use my method to produce some canisters, and since now I've made some progress, can I tell the rest of the team about it so they can start using my canisters for their efforts in finding a cure?"

"No, Chandor. This is top secret. We don't want this falling into the wrong hands, do we? National security is paramount, and I'm the Chancellor of Clidurna. I think the safest place to store the canisters is in my vault."

"But how are my teammates going to use the canisters for experimentation to develop the cure? You said that was what they'd be used for," Chandor rebutted.

"Chandor, all that will come in due course. First we need you to produce a stockpile. Then, it needs to be stored safely, and what safer place to store it than the best guarded place in Clidurna, the Chancellor's residence? Surely, you must know, even though you've just arrived, that I'm the foremost guardian of Clidurna's interest by virtue of my position."

Chandor wondered if there was a way for him to get out of this conundrum. Unable to think of any in a quick moment, Chandor felt that he had no choice but to lie to pacify Crull for the time being.

"Yes, sure, I'm sure the Chancellor's vault is the safest place in all Clidurna." *Except when it seems that the Chancellor is the one plotting some monkey business*, Chandor thought.

"I'm glad you agree, Chandor. You catch on fast. So, when can you produce your first batch of 10 canisters and deliver them over to me? I'm guessing since you can produce them in a day, you can probably deliver them by the day after?"

"Don't you want me to produce a bit more, then deliver it all together at once?" Chandor tried to stall for time.

"No, we don't want to risk a lack of security at your lab. Here's safer. So you've said you can produce 10 in a day, right?"

"Yes, about that amount."

"So here's what you're going to do. You will produce as much as you can tomorrow, if it's a few shy of 10, that's all right. Then we'll arrange for somebody from the armed forces to pick it up from your office, all right? That's more secure and it'll save you the trip here."

"Uh, yeah, sure."

"But first, we want the formulas for developing this substance. It's in your communicator, I presume?"

Chandor did not want to divulge it, least of all to Crull, whom he felt he could not trust now. "Yes, but you know, it's all chemical engineering gobbledygook. You wouldn't want to try and make sense of it yourself."

"That doesn't matter. Fire it up."

Chandor hesitated. At that moment, all eyes were on him. He felt trapped.

Feeling that he was left with no option, Chandor ordered his communicator to show the plans for his method holographically.

"Beautiful. Don't you think so, guys?" Crull addressed Bink and Clobb.

"Certainly. I'm no chemical engineer but just by first impressions, it seems pretty detailed. Must be a fine piece of work."

"OK, Chandor. Transfer it over to my communicator now." Crull gave him a smile.

Not wanting to raise Crull's suspicions, Chandor complied, his heart beating fast. He hoped a transmission error would somehow occur.

"Transmission complete," the communicator's voice called out. Chandor's heart sank.

Thankfully for Chandor, the plans were not entirely complete yet and part of the plans were in no other place except his own brain. Nevertheless, he was sure that a skilled chemical engineer, perhaps Thurl or one of his teammates if ordered to do so, would be able to work out the missing parts.

"Excellent, Chandor. We're done here, now, aren't we, guys?" Crull seemed eager to draw the meeting to a close.

"Yup, nothing further from me," replied Bink with a broad smile.

"Nor me," Clobb added, smiling as well.

"Great. So Chandor, why don't you go back and get cracking and produce the 10 canisters we want. Great job you've done so far. With such speed, I'm sure our research is going to pay off really soon."

Chandor went back into the capsule, his mind spinning. He wondered what all of that about the members of the opposition being real pests, and what that had to do with the canisters. It seemed downright sinister, and he wondered if Crull was such a maniac that he would be plotting murder, and why. He had to find out.

VII.   Framed

Chandor returned to Lunasilico, thinking of what best to do. The plans for the production of the canisters were now in Crull's hands, except for some parts which he had not drafted yet. Those would be easily filled in by any competent chemical engineer, such as one of his colleagues. They would do the job, not knowing about Crull's potential plans to deal with some members of the opposition who were "real pests".

Chandor was puzzled, however, as to why Crull might go to the extent of plotting murder. He thought it best to ask Thurl more about the political situation in Clidurna.

Chandor knocked on Thurl's office door and went in.

"Chandor, hi. How did your meeting with Crull go?"

"It was fine, but I've been told not to tell anyone about what I'm doing, including our team."

Thurl laughed. "Don't worry about that. That's normal. Here in Lunasilico, we do all sorts of hush-hush stuff."

"Can I ask you a question?"

"Sure."

"What does the opposition do in Clidurna? Are relations bad between the opposition and government in Clidurna?"

Thurl raised an eyebrow quizzically and laughed. "That's odd. Why are you suddenly interested in Clidurnian politics?"

"Just wondering, you know."

"So, Clidurna is a multi-party democracy as you know. With a parliamentary system. The Chancellor is indirectly elected by parliamentarians. After every general election the parties generally form up into 2 large coalitions, 1 being the governing coalition and the other being the opposition coalition. The parties who are not in government get to elect a Leader of the Opposition.

Of course, like in any typical rambunctious democracy, the opposition and government disagree with each other a fair bit. In our history, there have even been rather silly fights in the parliamentary chamber before. Once, they had a food fight and threw food at each other. Another time, they used water guns used for rehydrating food to spray each other. Sometimes, politicians are like overgrown children." Thurl chuckled.

"Are there any opposition politicians who have a bad relationship with Crull?"

"Well, of course in any democracy there is bound to be disagreement. I don't think Crull takes it against them personally. But I do know that Crull is not on particularly good terms with the current Leader of the Opposition."

"And why is that?" asked Chandor.

"Well, as you know Clidurna is somewhat suspicious of Blissaune. We don't have any trading relationship with Blissaune. We don't even have formal immigration controls with Blissaune - anyone who needs to travel there does so on an ad-hoc basis, and needs a special permit. But the Leader of the Opposition wants to change that. He wants to start some kind of trading relationship with Blissaune."

"So that's why Crull doesn't like the Leader of the Opposition?"

"Well, there's more. Crull tried to pass a law quite a while ago, which was intended to give him emergency powers, ostensibly to deal with spies from Blissaune after Blissaune was suspected of the sabotage in Lintal, something you're intimately aware of. The Leader of the Opposition orchestrated a protest, saying that the laws were dictatorial and an overreach of Crull's authority. As it went, enough parliamentarians from the governing coalition were convinced to vote against that law. So Crull didn't manage to get it passed in the end. I was actually quite pleased about that. Don't get me wrong, I get along fine with Crull. But I did think that the law he was proposing was rather too draconian. Crull was quite angry about the whole affair, I remember."

"Do you think Crull is still unhappy? Would he do anything about it?"

"Heavens no!" Thurl smiled. "I don't think anyone would bear a grudge for that long. But it's politics, he'll probably think of something to make the other side look bad, something like that. It happens all the time."

If only you'd heard what I heard, thought Chandor. *Or am I getting too suspicious? Maybe the production of the canisters isn't linked to Crull seeing the opposition members as pests?*

Chandor went back to work, wondering whether he should produce the 10 canisters or not. If he did not, Crull would probably be angered by his refusal. If he did, he was afraid that Crull would use them for some illegitimate purpose.

In the end, Chandor decided that he would produce 10 dummy canisters, which would emit a relatively harmless dust which would cause nothing but some coughing. He worked on them quickly. Chandor also backed up his plans for the actual rapid silicosis inducing dust into a fingernail drive (the successor of the thumb drive, and a far tinier device), then deleted it from his own communicator and the Lunasilico servers.

In no time, Chandor had produced 10 dummy canisters from the lab. He rang Crull on the communicator.

"Hi Crull. The jobs done. How do I get the canisters over to you?"

"Wow, you're fast, Chandor! I'll send some police officers to pick it up from you. It's too dangerous for you to bring something like that over to my office yourself. Just sit tight and wait where you are," Crull responded.

"Right, I'll be waiting in the lab at Lunasilico."

Chandor sat in the lab, nervous beyond words, waiting for the police officers to come and collect the dummy canisters. He hoped this ruse would work.

Some time later, 2 police officers arrived. "Chandor?"

"Yes. I've got the stuff right here."

"10 of them, right?" the police officer handed the canisters over to her colleague who started counting them.

"Yes."

The police officer's colleague nodded.

"Thanks a lot, Chandor. You're making a great contribution to Clidurna with your work," the first police officer said.

Chandor nodded. "Just doing my job."

The police officers left, bringing the canisters with them.

~

Over the next few days, Chandor watched the news on his communicator every night with bated breath, waiting to see if the canisters were indeed going to be used for any abnormal purposes.

Finally, about 3 days later, it hit the news.

"The Leader of the Opposition has taken ill with a mild coughing fit after a suspicious canister containing an unidentified powder was released in his office. Police have identified a suspect who may be the culprit. It is not known if this was a prank or a botched attempt at serious sabotage. We have Inspector Clidd here with us. What have the police investigations shown, Inspector?" asked the news anchor.

"We've examined the canister for fingerprints. We don't know why this was done, and whether it was just a prank, but we're taking this seriously and not leaving anything to chance. We suspect that a foreign operative was involved. The prime suspect, based on the forensic evidence, is a male working at Lunasilico, a recent immigrant from Lintal…"

Oh shoot, that's me. I'm being framed, thought Chandor.

"We don't have clearance to release his name yet, but we're monitoring his every move and will probably call him to assist in investigations soon."

Chandor turned off the news in disbelief. It was Crull's doing, he was sure of that, and now Crull was trying to sic it on him. Thankfully, he had not delivered the actual substance, otherwise he would now be a murder suspect. He couldn't believe that he was so stupid to not have realised that his fingerprints would be all over the canisters, being the last person who was working on them. Thinking back, he seemed to recall that the 2 police officers collecting the canisters were wearing gloves. Perhaps they were crooked and in the know as well.

Chandor thought about his chances of survival if he were to remain in Clidurna, and he felt his prospects were bleak. His ruminations were interrupted by a call on his communicator.

It was Thurl. "So, Chandor. I guess you've heard the news."

"Yes, I have."

"Well, I'm not sure what exactly is going on here, but I've received a courtesy call from the police saying that they'll be coming over to Lunasilico tomorrow to ask you some questions. Well, I have every reason to believe there might be a misunderstanding somewhere and I'd advise you to cooperate as much as you can. Don't try to run away because that's just going to make things worse; they're watching you round the clock and you haven't a snowball's chance in hell of slipping through their grasp. They've been nice enough to give me a courtesy call, so do yourself and everyone a favour, just turn up to work tomorrow as usual and cooperate with the police investigation, all right?"

"Right."

"Great, I knew I could count on you." Thurl hung up.

Chandor had a fitful sleep, not knowing what the next day would have in store.

The next day, Chandor followed Thurl's advice and turned up at work as usual. When he arrived, there were 2 strangers standing at his desk, together with Thurl. Thurl had his lips pursed and looked uncomfortable.

"Is this Chandor?" one of the strangers asked Thurl.

Thurl nodded.

"Chandor, we're from the Clidurnian police."

"Yes, and you're here to ask me some questions, right?"

"Erm, not quite." The police officer paused before continuing. "You have the right to remain silent. Anything you say can and will be used against you. You have the right to talk to a lawyer for advice before we ask you any questions. You have the right to have a lawyer with you during questioning. If you cannot afford a lawyer, one will be appointed for you before any questioning if you wish. If you decide to answer questions now without a lawyer present, you have the right to stop answering at any time. Now that we've read you your rights, Chandor, you're under arrest and we have instructions to take you into custody."

"Huh?" Bewildered, Chandor shot a look at Thurl.

"Sorry, Chandor. I didn't know about this until they came here today. Up till they told me just now, I was under the impression that they would just want to question you here."

Chandor's pulse raced as he thought of how he could get out of this mess. "I'm innocent," he said, not knowing what else to say.

"You can tell us more at the lockup," one of the police officers responded.

"Go with them, Chandor. Guys, I believe Chandor will cooperate." Thurl looked at the police officers.

"Sure, unless he struggles, I don't think hand immobilisers will be necessary."

The 2 police officers grabbed Chandor by the shoulders. Chandor instinctively wriggled free of their grasp.

"I guess the hand immobilisers are necessary. Sorry." One of the police officers produced a tiny device, similar to the one used in Lintal, and Chandor's hands were instantly and violently attracted together behind him.

"Ow!" cried Chandor.

"We told you not to struggle," the police officer's colleague added, somewhat sympathetically.

"Go along with them, Chandor. We have rights here in Clidurna. It won't be as bad as in Lintal," Thurl said to Chandor.

"I can't believe this is happening again." Chandor fumed.

The police officers led Chandor away, through the corridors of Lunasilico. Chandor's teammates and other colleagues in Lunasilico gawked.

"I'm sure you'll be alright, Chandor!" Kaylor cried out as he passed her.

Well, at least it seems 1 person here believes in me, thought Chandor. He couldn't believe his rotten luck, and wished that he had never once decided to move to the moon. He had never been arrested or even stopped by the police for so much as a traffic incident back on earth. Now that he was on the moon, he had been detained twice by the cops.

~

The police officers brought him straight to an interview room in the lockup. "Somebody really important is going to interview you," one of the police officers said.

"Who? The chancellor?" Chandor snickered.

The police officer looked surprised. "How did you guess?"

"Who else could it be but the mastermind of all this nonsense?"

"Now, you'd best be careful there. Don't go around accusing anyone of anything, any old how. Mind you, we have laws against you making such allegations, especially against somebody as important as the Chancellor."

"What if I tell you he's the one behind all this?"

"I don't care what you want to say. You can say it to the Chancellor himself." The police officer left the room.

After a while, Crull entered the room.

"Recording off," he announced immediately to turn off the automated holographic video recorder.

"So, Chandor. We meet again," Crull continued.

"Yes, and I'm glad I foiled your dastardly plan."

"Or rather, you think you may have. Don't forget, you transferred me the formula. Any chemical engineer with half a brain can piece together what you left out."

"But no one will do it. Not after I've outed you for how you framed me."

"Framed? No, no, don't you remember? Your fingerprints were found all over the canister discovered in the room of the Leader of the Opposition. Mine weren't. Why would I want to play such a prank on my parliamentary colleague? Or rather, it wasn't a prank, but a botched attempted murder, wasn't it? Do you think the public and the Court would believe me, Chancellor of Clidurna, or you, a suspicious foreigner, ejected from Lintal in ignominious circumstances?" Crull gave a sinister laugh.

"Well, why would I want to do anything to the Leader of the Opposition? You're the one with a motive for harming him."

"Really, Chandor? You are obviously a foreign operative, probably a spy. You came to the moon from earth all of a sudden, moved to Lintal, then met with some strangers, and soon thereafter got booted out of Lintal and ended up here. You think people won't find that you have a suspicious background? Chandor, Chandor - you're untrustworthy, otherwise I could have helped you if you actually gave me the real goods instead of pulling a fast one on me."

Chandor ignored Crull's baiting. "What I don't understand is, why did you go to the extent of plotting murder against the Leader of the Opposition? Sure, he opposes your embargo on Blissaune, and he didn't support the law giving you emergency powers, but did you have to kill him to achieve your purposes? You're the Chancellor after all. You'll get your way eventually."

"Chandor, Chandor. Are you really that naive? You know that Clidurna has term limits and a whole load of restrictions on what the Chancellor can do, don't you? Do you really think that I wanted the emergency laws just to deal with Blissaune spies? *Au contraire*, if I had passed that law, what couldn't I do in Clidurna then? I could arrest anyone on the grounds that they were suspected Blissaune operatives. Then Clidurna would be mine for life."

"You're a piece of trash. So much for Clidurna being a supposed democracy."

"It is one now, unfortunately. But it won't be for long. After we deal with you, foreign spy, I'll make sure everybody knows the importance of having emergency legislation allowing for detention without trial. Then we can begin to be strong, without me being hampered by all these processes and Opposition and whatnot. Democracy is for the weak," Crull sneered. "Look at Blissaune - they can just do whatever they want, and that's why they're the strongest among the 3 states militarily."

"So what's the purpose of talking to me now? Just to reveal your plans? Not afraid I'll tell everyone about them?"

"I'm afraid not, Chandor. Because as is normal procedure for any serious criminal charge, you will be assessed for insanity by a psychiatrist. If you're found insane, you won't face trial, poor you. You'll instead be sent to a mental health facility to be detained indefinitely for treatment, all for your own good. And you know what, Chandor - I'm no psychiatrist, but all that nonsense about me being the mastermind of an evil plot makes you sound like you're insane to me. And I'm quite certain you will be certified insane. So poor you, we care for people like you and won't put you on trial - you'll get long-term mental health treatment courtesy of the taxpayers of Clidurna instead." Crull threw his head back and cackled.

Chandor felt his heart beating rapidly upon hearing that. He wondered if there was a way out.

"Enjoy your stay here, Chandor. We treat our inmates well. We treat our mental patients well, too, but be warned - mental patients who are out of control get secured fast to their bed and immobilised. And I hear you're pretty out of control, struggling with the police and all that. Goodbye, Chandor." Crull gave him a sideways glance and a sinister smile, then left the room.

The police officers came in and brought Chandor to a cell in the lockup. Chandor couldn't believe that this was being done to him. The way Crull had said it, it sounded like he had already bribed the doctor, or something like that, to certify that he was insane so that the truth would never come out. Chandor wondered what he could do to get the truth out if he were indeed sent for a psychiatric assessment.

~

Several hours passed for Chandor in the lockup with nobody coming to interrogate him. He was in a cell of his own as he was considered a security risk. He was not given access to any lawyer. Chandor was bored to tears with nothing to do all day long.

The next day, a police officer came in. "Get up," he commanded. "You're going for a psychiatric assessment."

Odd as it was, Chandor was looking forward to it, as he would finally have something to do. He hoped that he could convince the psychiatrist to let him tell his story in Court.

VIII.   Kidnapped

Chandor was led with his hands secured behind his back down a series of narrow travellators.

"So, what's the psychiatric assessment going to be like?" he asked the police officer.

"I don't know, and even if I did, I'm not going to tell you anything. I've heard about you, you're the one coming up with a crazy conspiracy theory saying the Chancellor is behind all this. I hope they put you away for a long time in the loony bin," the police officer remarked.

"Do you just always believe everything you've been told all the time?" asked Chandor quizzically.

"I believe what's credible. You, sir, are not," the police officer retorted.

Making no headway, Chandor decided to remain quiet for the rest of the ride.

All of a sudden…

BOOM!

An enormous explosion shook the walls of the travellator tube that Chandor was in.

Both Chandor and the police officer were stunned and dived to the ground.

The next thing Chandor knew, strong hands were pulling him up.

"Whhaatt?" Chandor managed to mumble.

The hands, which felt too strong to be human hands, continued pulling Chandor along. Smoke billowed everywhere, and Chandor could barely see ahead of him.

Glad it seems I can still breathe, thought Chandor. *Guess they didn't blow a hole right through the roof to outer space, else all our air would have leaked out and everyone would be dead.*

Chandor was plopped onto what seemed like an electronic skateboard as he and the other 2 persons whizzed along various hidden passageways until they got to a ramp that led high into the sky. They went up the ramp and eventually found themselves in a small spacecraft. Once inside, the two persons dragging Chandor sat in the front seats and left Chandor in the back seat. The spacecraft took off.

"Who are you?" asked Chandor, bewildered.

"We're Special Forces troopers from Blissaune. Clidurna's sworn enemies, or so they'd have everyone believe," one of the two persons who dragged him answered.

"Where are you bringing me? What are you doing to me?"

"We're bringing you to Blissaune, of course. Our intelligence found out that you'd been locked up. Can't let that happen to you. Don't worry, we came to rescue you," the other trooper answered.

Chandor could see that they were both wearing a powered exoskeleton. *That explains their immense strength*, he thought.

"But why would you rescue me?" Chandor asked, puzzled.

"Our intelligence found out about what you were doing, of course. We know about what happens everywhere. What you have created might be of immense use. Once we heard that Clidurna had thrown you in jail, we thought your talents might be best used in the service of Blissaune," the male trooper sitting in the left front seat of the spacecraft replied.

"And if I refuse?"

The female trooper sitting in the right front seat of the spacecraft laughed. "Trust me, you won't want to refuse."

"Whyever not?"

"We have our ways," she answered. The answer sent a chill down Chandor's spine. He had already been scapegoated and imprisoned by 2 of the countries on the moon, and those were supposedly democracies. He shuddered to think what might happen to him in Blissaune.

Chandor wondered how his life had turned topsy-turvy all of a sudden, since he had come to the moon. He had been arrested not once, but twice, when he had never been arrested before on earth. Each time, the arrest had resulted in him being completely uprooted from his previous environment. At least the transition from Lintal to Clidurna was somewhat smoother, with things being arranged for him, Thurl meeting him at the border and him getting a refund for his residence. Now, he had nothing except the clothes on his back.

A jolt snapped Chandor out of his thoughts. He heard whirring noises outside the spacecraft. *We must be docking*, he thought.

"We're here. Welcome to Blissaune," said one of the troopers.

Some welcome, Chandor thought, as they exited the spacecraft.

Chandor came out to a gleaming gold spaceport, ornate but gaudy at the same time. It looked like it was built by someone with delusions of grandeur and a distinctly offbeat taste.

"First thing, you're going to have an audience with the King. Consider yourself lucky. Many Blissauneans never even meet the King in person in their entire lives," remarked one of the troopers.

They led him to a travelator. Chandor found it interesting how some things were the same on the moon regardless of where one was. The use of travelators was one of those things.

"Why are there so few people in the spaceport?" Chandor asked.

"This is a private spaceport. The royal spaceport. What, did you think an ordinary spaceport would be built of gold?"

"No wonder," mused Chandor.

They continued down a series of travelators and elevators and went through several doors, and then they were there.

"Here. It's the palace," the female trooper said in a hushed tone.

They approached the door, which had 2 people standing on each side.

"Identify yourselves!" one of the persons boomed.

"Troopers Milth and Mowd, bringing the subject Chandor."

"Enter!" the 2 people manually swung the doors open.

Chandor was surprised. "Wow, are there actually real human doormen here? It's not automated?"

"You wouldn't think a King would deign to settle for just some automated security system like a common man, would you?" replied the male trooper.

"An actual hinged door too, not your typical automated sliding door. Your king is quite the history buff."

The trooper made no reply. They led Chandor into the room, where he saw a man sitting on a gold throne decorated with all manner of carvings.

"Your Majesty. Troopers Milth and Mowd. We have succeeded in our mission to bring the subject Chandor to Blissaune. Here he is," the female trooper addressed the king.

"Ah, what have we here?" The king rubbed his hands. "A fine specimen of humanity, no doubt. Welcome to Blissaune, Chandor. The journey wasn't too hard on you I hope?"

"Well I guess anything beats being stuck in a Clidurnian lockup. My life has been so full of upheavals recently, I'm kind of getting used to feeling disconnected from my surroundings."

"I trust our royal troopers have told you why you're here?"

"No, as a matter of fact, they haven't."

"You're a smart guy, Chandor. Guess?"

"You want the deadly chemical," Chandor stated simply.

"There! I knew you'd know. It hasn't got a name?"

"No, it hasn't got a name."

"Well, since it turns the face blue, let's call it Blueface. How's that?" The king looked at the troopers beside him.

"Excellent idea, sire!"

"An ingenious name, sire!"

Chandor rolled his eyes in disbelief. *Sycophants*, he thought, *this "king" they have is an absolute caricature of a tinpot dictator.*

"You rolled your eyes, Chandor. Don't think I didn't notice that," the king frowned at him, staring at him with beady eyes.

"On earth, that's a compliment, sire. We earthlings have a different culture. And of course, it's a most creative name, sire. Only someone of your stature could come up with it," Chandor replied hastily, deciding that it was best to preserve his life in an unfamiliar land.

"Aha! You catch on quick. I knew you would. Someone of your calibre would fit right in in Blissaune. So, you're going to create Blueface for us?"

"I haven't agreed yet, sire."

"No worries! You will in due course. Everyone comes around eventually."

Like hell I will, thought Chandor.

"Milth and Mowd, bring him to his quarters. Now, Chandor, I believe you had an apartment in Clidurna, but you'll find things here better than ever."

"Sure beats the lockup, I guess."

The king laughed. "You bet. Now, you'll be on your way."

Milth and Mowd led Chandor out of the chamber into the hallway again. They led him out of a series of travelators. Then, to Chandor's surprise, they stopped at a flight of stairs and Milth and Mowd took a first step up.

"Stairs?" Chandor exclaimed.

"Yes, never seen them before?" said the female trooper.

"I've seen them before on earth, sure, but isn't it the case that nobody uses them anymore?"

"Not here. Only the king and government buildings have elevators. The rest of us use stairs elsewhere. What, you think you're too good for climbing stairs?" asked the male trooper.

"Well, I guess I haven't got a choice, have I?" Chandor asked rhetorically.

"Glad you know you haven't," responded the female trooper. Chandor followed them up the stairs, feeling weird. He had never climbed stairs in his life before because he had to. There were stair-climbing competitions he took part in on earth, but those were for athletic purposes. He couldn't believe that normal people didn't have elevators in Blissaune.

"So which of you is Milth and which of you is Mowd?"

"I'm Milth and she's Mowd," the male trooper answered.

"How did you come to be in Blissaune?" Chandor couldn't believe that anyone would choose to live in Blissaune voluntarily of their own accord.

"We're both Blissaunean born and bred," replied Mowd.

That explains it, Chandor thought. *But why did their parents come to Blissaune?*

Chandor verbalised his thoughts. "Why did your parents come to Blissaune?"

The trio stopped outside a door. "Now, that's enough questions for today," said Mowd, "We're here. Here's your key. You'll be staying here until further notice."

"Key? You mean the door doesn't identify me automatically?"

"Yes, it doesn't. You have to use a key. We all use keys in Blissaune," said Milth.

Chandor looked at the key. *Wow, that looks like one of those Thumb Drives used in old computers that they have in the history museum on earth*, he thought.

"Right, we'll be off then. Don't try anything funny. We'll be back tomorrow at 9:00 AM GMT. If we don't find you here, you can guess what might happen to you," said Mowd.

"What do I do with this key?"

Milth looked at him like Chandor was stupid. "You put it in the door, of course. Then it opens." Milth pointed to a hole in the door.

"Right, of course."

Milth and Mowd left.

Chandor placed the key in the hole in the door. The door swung open. Yet another hinged door. Chandor ceased to be surprised by now. Blissaune was like a living museum. It was like earth in the 2020s.

Chandor stepped into the apartment, not knowing what to expect. He thought he might find a dark, dingy room, covered with cobwebs.

It was a bit of an anticlimax when the lights of the apartment came on. While the style looked somewhat dated, it looked like a normal apartment, not too different from the ones he had been in in Lintal and Clidurna. It had the style of an apartment on earth several years ago, with muted earth tones, beiges and browns all around. It looked clean enough.

Better than I expected, thought Chandor.

Having nothing to unpack, Chandor found some freeze-dried food in the fridge fixed himself a meal. He was glad that the water guns worked just the same as they did in Lintal and Clidurna. Chandor spent the rest of the settling into the apartment.

~

The next day, Chandor woke up early. It was some time before Milth and Mowd arrived at 9:00 AM sharp.

"Get moving, we're going to see His Majesty again," said Milth.

"Right, of course."

Chandor followed Milth and Mowd down the stairs, still feeling somewhat unused to them.

They headed down the same series of travelators as the day before, in the reverse direction. They arrived back at the palace chamber that they were in the day before.

"Chandor is here again, sire," Milth informed the king.

There was an unfamiliar woman sitting beside the king.

"Good to see you again, Chandor. Have you had a good rest?"

"As good as can be had in unfamiliar surroundings, sire."

"Great. Let me introduce you to my daughter, Celith." He gestured towards the unfamiliar woman, who angled her head slightly. Celith had a tiara on her head and wore a flowing pink gown.

Like something out of a fantasy movie, thought Chandor.

"Pleased to make your acquaintance, Chandor," Celith said, interrupting Chandor's thoughts.

"And I yours, Celith."

"Audacious!" Milth hissed. "Princess Celith is to be addressed as Your Royal Highness!"

Chandor was somewhat startled by Milth's fierce tone.

"Not to worry, Milth. Chandor is not from Blissaune. He's not used to royal protocol," Celith replied smoothly.

"I beg your pardon, Your Royal Highness," Chandor said. *This is silly*, thought Chandor. *They aren't even from a long-established monarchy like some of those on earth. Just a bunch of robber barons who set themselves up as a royal family.*

"So, Chandor, let's get down to business. First of all, why don't you take a seat?" The king gestured towards a chair. Chandor sat.

"My daughter is here because she will be in charge of the Blueface project."

Chandor gave a quizzical look. "Do you have a chemical engineering background?" he asked Celith.

"I did learn some chemistry when I was in school, but of course, I would defer to an expert like you, Chandor," Celith answered.

"See, isn't my daughter wise." The king beamed.

I must stop this constant tendency of rolling my eyes, thought Chandor.

"What we want is for you to re-create Blueface here. We know you tricked your chancellor Crull. You were supposed to create a new batch of canisters, I believe, and you gave him dummies instead. And you didn't give him a complete blueprint."

"How do you know about everything that happened in Clidurna?"

"We have excellent intelligence, Chandor," the king replied.

Chandor was surprised that they would have excellent intelligence, seeing as Blissaune seemed to be backward in so many ways. *Perhaps they spend all their money on the military*, thought Chandor.

"What do you want Blueface for?" asked Chandor.

"Ah, let's not get there. Let's stick to what we know. We know you can create Blueface. We hear you're a genius, Chandor. It's all stored in your brain."

"But maybe I can't remember it anymore," Chandor tried.

"You expect me to believe that? You're taking me for a fool, Chandor," the king retorted. His lips curled into a thin smile. "You will be well rewarded, that's for certain, Chandor."

"What if I can't do it?" Chandor tried again.

"Chandor, Chandor. I'm afraid that if the carrot doesn't work, we'll have to use the stick then.

You're in our hands, Chandor. Do you think you can get out of our clutches?" The king looked at Chandor intently.

Perhaps he's not such a nincompoop after all, thought Chandor.

"So once I produce something for you, you'll let me go?" asked Chandor.

"Not so fast. We know you pulled a fast one on the Chancellor. So you will have create canisters that can release Blueface partially, so that we can test that every single one of them works. Then after that, we can talk about letting you go. But maybe you'll not want to go after all. After we give you all Blissaune has to offer, would you rather return to a Clidurnian prison?" The king asked Chandor, leaving no doubt as to the answer he wanted.

"I might still have some difficulty, sire. It's not just what you can answer it, it's whether I can in fact re-create what I created in Clidurna. I don't even know if we hae the needed equipment here." Chandor made a last-ditch attempt to wiggle out of the project.

The king shook his head gently. "We're going nowhere, Chandor. Well, since you say you might find it difficult, why don't you give it a try first. Follow Celith to the lab, and we'll see what you can do. Celith will keep me updated on whether she thinks you're using your best efforts. Celith, off to the labs. Bring him there, Milth and Mowd."

Milth and Mowd beckoned Chandor, and Chandor was marched off to the chemistry lab.

IX.   An unexpected discovery

As Chandor was escorted by Milth and Mowd to the chemistry lab, one of them on each side, with Celith walking ahead, he tried to make small talk with them again.

"So, why did you guys decide to become troopers, huh?"

"It's part of our tour of duty. Every Blissaunean is enlisted into the military for 5 years. It's an honour that we were selected to serve the crown in such a great way, as Special Forces troopers, as part of our military service," Milth said proudly.

Such a long period of mandatory military service, thought Chandor. *Almost as bad as that historical dictatorship on earth, North Korea.*

"Isn't 5 years kind of a long time?" asked Chandor.

"Not at all. Like Milth said, we are proud to serve the Blissaunean crown. It's a mark of our loyalty to His Majesty," Mowd answered swiftly.

Thoroughly brainwashed, thought Chandor.

They arrived at the door of the chemistry lab. Celith turned around.

"All right, Milth, Mowd, thanks for doing a great job bringing Chandor to Blissaune. We'll be sure to bestow a major award on both of you for this. I'll take it from here. You can report back to your unit."

"Glad to have done our duty, Your Royal Highness," Milth replied. Milth and Mowd turned to leave.

"Follow me in, Chandor," Celith said. Celith opened the door to the lab, yet another manually opened hinged door. Chandor was not too hopeful about the quality of the lab, and thought he might use that as an excuse for being unable to produce Blueface.

Chandor followed Celith in and she closed the door.

"Your Royal Highness…" Chandor began.

"OK, Chandor. Now that we're in private here, you can call me Celith."

"Wow, thanks. I'm guessing that's an immense privilege."

"To the average Blissaunean at least. Not to the people I know or I'm close to."

"We just met, though."

"Enough with the preliminaries. Chandor, tell me - what are you?"

"What do you mean, what am I?"

"How did you even end up here? How did you come to create Blueface? Why did you create Blueface?"

"I thought Blissaune's military intelligence was superb."

"Sometimes it is, sometimes it isn't. We never really know until we meet the person himself or herself. Are you going to answer my question, Chandor?"

Despite having only just met Celith, something about her forthright manner made Chandor decide to trust her.

Chandor told Celith the entire story of how he came from earth, got ejected from Lintal, came up with Blueface by accident and got arrested in Clidurna, then got kidnapped by the Blissaunean troopers.

"Wow, you've been through quite a lot in a very short time, haven't you," Celith remarked sympathetically when Chandor finished.

"You could say that, and even that's quite an understatement," added Chandor.

"Chandor. I know you don't want to create Blueface for my father. I can only guess what plans he might have once you give him a batch of Blueface, but I'm sure they're not good ones."

"Do I have a choice?" asked Chandor.

"My father won't monitor this project. He trusts me absolutely since I'm his daughter. But do you know something, Chandor?"

"What?"

"Can I trust you, Chandor?"

"Yes, of course - I've trusted you by telling you my life story. Well, just the part since I've landed on the moon."

"Alright. My father's trust in me is completely misplaced, because I'm a secret member of the Democratic Activists League. It's a group that's opposed to the current absolute monarchy. We haven't decided if we'll support retaining the monarchy in some form as a constitutional monarchy, or do away with it entirely."

Chandor was taken aback by this revelation. "But why would you do that? You're a princess. You have everything to gain by leaving the system in Blissaune as it is."

"Yes, that's if I was self-interested. Years ago, I couldn't care less. Everything was fine, I had a privileged position, I didn't understand why some people wanted change. But gradually, as I grew up, I realised that there was something disturbing about how my father maintained his power. This whole thing about getting you to recreate Blueface is, unfortunately, quite typical of him. Increasingly, I began to believe that his iron-fisted rule must come to an end. He portrays this image of an ignoramus, but he's a cunning man. There are people who have just disappeared for no reason, people sent to indoctrination camps who come out thoroughly brainwashed, and a lot of other disturbing things in Blissaune," Celith continued.

"So what do you want me to do now you've told me this?"

"Instead of creating Blueface for my father, I want you to continue working on the antidote. It's only a matter of time before Crull, or some chemical engineer working for him, hits on the formula and manages to re-create it without the missing parts which you hid from him. And it's only a matter of time before my father's other scientists either discover Blueface, given how you've told me it's very simple, conceptually, to create, or come up with some other lethal chemical. Either way, it would lead to chemical warfare on the moon - something Lintal, Clidurna and Blissaune can all ill afford to have. An arms race is the last thing we want to see. It would destroy the human community on the moon and set back humanity's lunar settlement project by a generation," she said passionately.

"That sounds sensible. Wow. But I'm surprised your father still trusts you and is willing to put you in charge of this. Does he have any idea you're part of an activist group seeking to dethrone him, or at least limit his powers?" asked Chandor.

"No, of course not. He has spies everywhere, and the secret police is a strong Blissaunean institution, as you might expect in a totalitarian state - but nobody dares to investigate me because I'm a princess. And whatever it is, no matter how much wrong I think my father has done, I still don't want any harm to come to him. Some of the more radical members of the group don't share that view. So it's a good thing that I'm in this group, because at least, if they do succeed, I can ensure my father's personal safety," replied Celith.

"That's a wise move of yours," remarked Chandor.

"So now, get cracking on the antidote. As you can tell, we don't really practice meritocracy here - I'm supervising you even though I haven't a clue about anything to do with chemical engineering. But supervise I must." Celith smiled at Chandor.

"You know I don't have any idea how to create it at all, right? I don't even know if we've got all the equipment."

"Well, our intelligence services found out that you used gas chromatography mass spectrometry and a particle accelerator to create Blueface, so we've got those. We've also got a small stockpile of moon dust, and some live rats for testing as well. As you can imagine, we've got nowhere near the level of expertise with moon dust as Clidurna, so that's the best we've got. But there's something about Blissaune that may interest you," answered Celith.

"What?"

"Well, Blissaune is primarily located on the dark side of the moon. We're around the site of the location where a gel-like substance on the moon was first discovered, and later discovered to be a form of glass. You probably know it's called impact-melt breccia. That's something that we have access to that Clidurna and Lintal don't. I don't have any idea if it'll be of any use to you, but I thought I'd let you know."

"Well, anything could help. Thanks for letting me know. Have you got any of that in your stores?" asked Chandor.

"Yes, we have collected some samples of impact-melt breccia. Everything we have can be retrieved from this lab. Feel free to look around. As you can see, the gas chromatography mass spectrometry machine's over there, and the particle accelerator as well. I'm supposed to watch you so I'll just stay in the lab, whenever you're here, to observe what you're doing. I'll be quiet as a mouse, unless you have something to ask me."

"Right, I'll get started then."

~

The next few days passed with Chandor settling into a routine. He woke up each day and headed to the lab. First, he managed to mix a small batch of Blueface for testing. The days passed with him trying to concoct various chemicals to test their reactions with Blueface.

He got to know Celith better as well, as she observed him everyday. Celith, despite being a princess, had a tumultuous childhood. In her infancy, the moon had not settled into its current political system of 3 separate *de facto* nations. At the time, her father had been fighting a war with various rival factions to gain control of Blissaune. In a way, Blissaune's development into an absolute monarchy was the result of a bitter civil war. While the states which had eventually become Lintal and Clidurna saw rival factions decide to settle their differences through a democratic political process, Blissaune's formation saw a great deal of intrigue and physical fights, even between family members.

"The fighting was not without rules, though, interestingly enough. Everybody knew that firearms were too dangerous to use on the moon and might result in everyone dying. So all parties agreed to refrain from the use of firearms. As a result, we saw lots of physical brawls and moon rocks being thrown at the opposing faction, literally. A bit like the dispute between China and India over border areas on earth, ages ago," Celith told Chandor.

"Wow, how old were you then?"

"Maybe about 5? But I remember everything. That's because the saddest moment in my life happened then. My mother died in one of the fights."

"Wow. That sounds tragic," Chandor said sympathetically.

"Yes. Well, you know back in ancient times on earth, women were not combatants in wars. With equality between the genders, that changed. As you know, in most wars since gender equality, women were also combatants, and hence fair targets as well. I guess that's a price to pay for equality. I was told my mother was a tough fighter, though, giving as good as she got. But moon rocks can be deadly even when thrown by hand."

"Sounds like Blissaune had a really violent history," Chandor remarked.

"You bet. Why d'you think my father's so paranoid? But I guess, sadly, to his peril, the only person he really trusts, me, is covertly against him."

"Don't you have siblings?"

"I'm an only child. They never had time to have more kids before my mother died, what with the war and all," replied Celith.

"Must have been a bit lonely growing up," remarked Chandor.

"Well it wasn't really that bad. I'm a bit of a loner anyway. I'm just glad that while women were seen as combatants and fair game just like men, children were still untouchable - otherwise I wouldn't even be alive. That was one of the surprisingly humane bits of the conflict."

"So it wasn't really the posh, mollycoddled childhood a princess is expected to have, eh?" Chandor teased.

"Oh, I was mollycoddled. Eventually. When finally my father's faction practically won the war and proclaimed him king, the other factions conceded and we've had relative peace ever since. And since then, I won't deny that being my father's daughter has its benefits. OK, back to work, Chandor. How's your progress?"

"Still testing some stuff. That glassy lunar regolith you mentioned? I think it's interesting."

"What about it?" Celith asked.

"It seems to have some reaction with Blueface, but I can't tell what its effects are yet."

"What reaction?"

"After I bombard it with meitnerium, it seems to cause Blueface to clump together, turning it into rock, so it can't spread as far. But it's not an antidote. It just stops Blueface from spreading through the air, it seems."

"Show me?"

Chandor brought out a small transparent airtight container with a small piece of lunar breccia in it. He threw in a small canister of Blueface into it, and locked the container. He pressed a button, and Blueface filled the container. Gradually, the Blueface seemed to settle and be attracted to the piece of lunar breccia.

"Seems to work, but very slow acting. Most of the Blueface is still in the air."

"Better not let my father know that you've managed to create Blueface again."

"Of course not, unless you tell him." Chandor laughed.

"And of course I'm not telling him," Celith laughed too.

As they both laughed, Chandor and Celith looked at each other. Their expressions turned serious. It had been several days which they had spent together already, and they were getting closer.

Then Celith leaned in and kissed Chandor.

Chandor was momentarily stunned and lost for words.

Celith blushed, then looked away and carried on as though she had not kissed Chandor at all.

~

A few more days passed, with Chandor carrying on his work. Celith did not talk about the awkward kiss, and neither did Chandor. Chandor watched the news everyday.

One day, a news article grabbed Chandor's attention.

"Mysterious deaths in Clidurna and Lintal.

The Leader of the Opposition in Clidurna was found dead in his home today in mysterious circumstances. His face and body had turned blue.

In similar circumstances, the President of Lintal was found dead in his office. His face and body had also turned blue.

Lintel is now in disarray, with the Vice-President, as the acting President, ordering an urgent investigation. The

Chancellor of Clidurna has declared a state of emergency in Clidurna.

'We have every reason to suspect that these acts were committed by a Blissaunean spy, named Chandor. He claimed to be from earth, was previously expelled from Lintal, and was also at one time in custody in Clidurna. He is believed to have created a dangerous chemical which kills instantaneously and turns the faces of those it kills blue. He escaped from custody in Clidurna through the actions of Blissaunean agents and is now believed to be at large in Blissaune. We will spare no effort in bringing this murderer to justice.'"

Chandor shook his head in disbelief. He could not believe that Crull had managed to re-create Blueface so soon after he left. He assumed that one or more of the other chemical engineers on his team had helped Crull to re-create Blueface. What was more outrageous was that Crull had found him a convenient target to frame again.

"I saw that," Celith remarked to Chandor.

"So now you know, I'm supposedly a wanted murderer."

"Except you're not, because it can't be you. You're here, and you couldn't have possibly committed the murders while you're here."

"Right, thanks for the vote of confidence," Chandor remarked sarcastically, "I'm sure the good people of Lintal and Clidurna would believe a Blissaunean about the innocence of a purported Blissaunean spy."

"Well, it's all the more urgent now that you come up with something to neutralise Blueface."

"I haven't been able to come up with an antidote to Blueface. As far as I can tell, it's fatal within minutes, with no cure. The best I can do thus far is using lunar breccia to attract Blueface to it. But it's too slow, it takes quite long before it absorbs all the Blueface in the air."

At that moment, Milth and Mowd entered the room.

"Your Royal Highness," announced Milth, "His Majesty would like to see Chandor at once."

"I bet this is something to do with the news articles. Your father probably believes that I can create Blueface already."

"We'll see. All right, Milth. We will go and see my father now."

X.   Time to save the moon

Milth and Mowd escorted Chandor and Celith back to the palace, where the king was waiting for them, sitting on his throne.

"Ah, Chandor! I don't know if you've seen the news, but it seems like you've gone gallivanting in Lintal and Clidurna and we hadn't even noticed you were missing!" The king chuckled.

Chandor was not quite as amused. "I have my suspicions on who was behind all this, Your Majesty."

"And who might that be? Not my daughter, I hope?" the king guffawed.

What a ridiculous man, thought Chandor. *How did he ever win the civil war and gain the throne? And if only he knew about what his daughter was up to.*

"Crull, Chancellor of Clidurna. The Leader of the Opposition was in favour of building ties with Blissaune, I was told. Crull was having none of it. Crull also wanted to control the whole of Clidurna. It looks like he's succeeded, given that he's now put Clidurna into a state of emergency and put all the blame on me," Chandor replied seriously.

"Ah, you think I didn't know that, Chandor? My dear boy, I've been on the throne for years. I always knew that Crull was a crafty one," the king added in a more serious tone.

Maybe he's not as addled as I thought he was, thought Chandor.

"So, Chandor. Now that we know Crull has his hands on the Blueface formula, when are **we** going to have it?" the king boomed. "For a genius of a chemical engineer like yourself, you seem to be taking an awfully long time to re-create something you created in the first place."

"Father. Chandor has been hard at work. He's tried everything possible, but he's nowhere near the formula yet," interjected Celith.

"Well, really, I must say I'm most perplexed at this lack of progress. How can we help him, Celith?"

"Meitnerium. He needs more of that. And more of that glassy lunar breccia. And perhaps more particle accelerators so he can speed up his experiments," Celith responded.

Chandor looked at Celith in surprise. He did not expect that Celith would know what to ask for. Then again, he had told her about what he had discovered about the lunar breccia.

"Very well then, you have full authority to get all that Chandor needs for him, Celith."

"Thank you, father."

"But I want to see progress. Chandor, by next week, you'll have some results for me, won't you?"

"I will do my best, Your Majesty," Chandor replied, "Of course, with Her Royal Highness' help."

"Right, back to work, then. Milth and Mowd, send them back to the labs."

~

Back in the privacy of the lab, Chandor asked Celith, "So what are we going to do? Your father wants results in a week. What's he going to do to me if I don't give him anything then?"

"Your guess is as good as mine, but I sure think it wouldn't be pretty. At least, he doesn't seem to suspect that you've already managed to re-create it, as we know you have."

"And I wonder what's going on in Clidurna and Lintal now, especially now that Crull has murdered not just the leader of the Clidurnian opposition, but the President of Lintal as well. I wonder why he did that, though."

"I believe we have our answer. You haven't seen the latest news, have you?" Celith looked at Chandor quizzically.

"No, I haven't," Chandor answered.

Celith displayed a holographic video from her communicator.

"Lintal and Clidurna are in a historic merger. Here are Chancellor Crull from Clidurna and Vice-President and Acting President of Lintal,

Lurth, making a historic announcement." announced the communicator.

"We are living in tumultuous times. Danger lurks in every corner. 2 lives have been lost. And these are 2 very important people in Clidurna and Lintal - the leader of the opposition of Clidurna, and the President of Lintal," said Vice-President Lurth.

"It is unprecedented, but in the face of a common enemy, our democracies have to be united. Lintal and Clidurna share a common democratic heritage. This distinguishes them from Blissaune, a totalitarian dictatorship."

"We have tolerated Blissaune for a long time, with its pretensions at being a monarchy, regarding its rulers as royalty and all that. Blissaune had, for the longest time, left Lintal and Clidurna largely alone, safe for brief instances of sabotage which were easily put down. But the death of our President and Clidurna's leader of the opposition, believed to be the acts of the Blissaunean operative Chandor, are the last straw."

"It is with a heavy heart that I declare that Lintal and Clidurna shall be united as one, in a state of emergency, and I shall wholly cede Lintal's sovereignty to the leadership of Chancellor Crull of Clidurna in the face of the assault by our Blissaunean enemies. We shall demand justice from Blissaune, and if they do not yield, there shall be war!"

Chandor looked at Celith, stunned.

"Things have moved quickly, indeed," Celith looked back at him. "He's a puppet," Celith said, reading Chandor's thoughts. "Crull has had this planned all along. The vice-president of Lintal must have been his ally from the start. His plan was to create an excuse to force a union with Lintal, so that he could control both Lintal and Clidurna. And then he needed a *casus belli* to invade Blissaune. This is his perfect opportunity."

"I never thought Crull would be so crafty," said Chandor, "And now I'm public enemy number 1 all over again. What will your father do? Will he hand me over to Crull?"

"You can bet your life he won't, not until you produce Blueface for him." She smiled. "Until then, you're indispensable. But I won't let you produce Blueface for him. Now that there's going to be a war, my father has probably got more dastardly uses for Blueface planned. We can't let him massacre innocent people on the moon. What we need now is the antidote, and fast."

"Back to square one again. I still haven't worked out the antidote. But what if we can use the lunar breccia to neutralise existing stores of Blueface that Crull might have?"

"That's a useful thought, but you've got to make it faster acting. If you can make it work faster, we might be able to get our operatives into Clidurna to destroy the stores that Crull has."

"Well, I guess I've got to put my nose to the grindstone until I find a solution."

~

The next few days passed with an even greater urgency. Chandor spent as much time as he could in the lab. Celith had managed to requisition for him more Meitnerium, lunar breccia and an additional particle accelerator which made it quicker for him to conduct experiments.

Finally, he hit the nail on the head and found what he thought was the correct proportion of Meitnerium to use on the lunar breccia.

"Look at this," he told Celith as he dropped a lump of lunar breccia bombarded with Meitnerium into a transparent airtight container, then sealed it with a tiny canister of Blueface inside, together with a live rat.

Chandor pressed a button and Blueface was released from the tiny canister. The rat began to cough and choke as usual and its face gradually turned blue.

However, slowly but surely, small dust particles began to appear to be attracted to the lump of lunar breccia in the container. They began to visibly clump together in the air and form a white residue on the piece of lunar breccia.

The rat coughed a few more times, then it began to move about as previously. While the rat's face still looked a bit blue, it was alive!

"We did it! The rat's saved!" cried Chandor.

"You're amazing, Chandor!" exclaimed Celith as she gave him a tight hug, then looked into his eyes.

"Are you going to kiss me again?" Chandor asked.

"You think you deserve it?" Celith asked playfully.

"I think *you* deserve it, for being by my side all this while. We've been so close to each other all this time. I've been wondering how to take things further since that last kiss."

Without another word, Chandor pulled Celith into his arms and kissed her.

~

"Now, we've got to figure out who's Crull's next target," Chandor told Celith.

"That's if he has a next target," Celith replied. "Crull's already got his perfect excuse for invading Blissaune. He might not need a next target."

"But I don't think that's like Crull at all. Remember, he wanted me to produce an entire batch of canisters. He probably got whoever it was in my team who has figured it out to produce lots more spare canisters for him. I don't think he'll stop at murdering 2 people."

"So who do you think is his next target?"

"I think it's probably somebody in Blissaune."

"But that doesn't make sense. Why would he want to do that when he's trying to blame Blissaune for all the sabotage that he's doing?"

"He's trying to make me the scapegoat. He'll paint a picture of me being a rogue Blissaunean, who after poisoning leaders of both Lintal and Clidurna, now turned on Blissaune itself. He'll use that as a justification to Blissauneans so that Blissauneans will welcome him to hunt me down as a rogue agent. In the process, he'll have Blissaune cede control to him. I think his wish is to take over the moon."

"But why would Blissauneans cede control to him?" Celith wondered aloud.

"He will probably target somebody high value. Once that high value target is down, Blissauneans will panic. Crull can portray himself as the potential saviour of Blissaune, in addition to Lintal and Clidurna, and control the entire moon."

"That means, his target is my…"

"Father." Celith and Chandor said at the same time.

"We have to warn him, and fast," said Chandor.

"We'll have to put your Blueface-neutralising breccia to use. But the problem is, once we let him know about that, he'll know that you've already managed to create Blueface again here. Otherwise, how'd you have tested it? And once he knows that you can create Blueface, he'll force you to produce it. I know what my father is like," said Celith soberly.

"Is there someone you trust, whom we can put on alert in case there's any assassination attempt on your father?"

"There is someone, a senior royal guard commander. He's like an uncle to me and he adores me. I'll call him on my communicator now and see if I can introduce you to him."

Celith started the call on her communicator and soon, a hologram of a middle aged man appeared.

"Celith! I'm always pleased to see you," the figure greeted them.

Chandor was somewhat surprised that the man did not address Celith as "Royal Highness". *Well, she did say he was like an uncle to her,* he thought.

"Uncle Clour! It's good to see you too. Can I introduce you to Chandor?"

"Ah, he needs no introduction," Clour said, "The well-known chemical engineering genius whom your father has had the wisdom to bring to our lands."

"You flatter me, Uncle Clour." Chandor figured that since Celith addressed him as uncle, he might as well do so as well.

"So, to what do I owe the honour of this call?" Clour turned towards Celith.

"Well, I'm sure you've heard about the goings-on in Lintal and Clidurna," Celith began.

"You think something might happen here as well?" Clour butted in before she could continue.

Wow, this guy is sharp, thought Chandor.

"We're afraid of the possibility. We fear somebody might make an assassination attempt on my father. We suspect Crull, the Chancellor of Clidurna, is behind all of this nonsense."

"The Clidurnian are always behind some sort of nonsense or other," Clour practically snorted. "But I'm more worried about the Democratic Activists League. Those rabble rousers might be in cahoots with the Clidurnian."

Chandor shot a look at Celith. Clearly, Clour, trusted as he was, did not know of Celith's own involvement in the Democratic Activists League.

"Uncle Clour, what we know is that Crull is likely to be in possession of what we call Blueface. Have you heard of that?"

"Oh, of course, that's why our friend Chandor here was brought over to Blissaune, wasn't it? So they managed to create it without him being there, did they?" Clour asked.

"Yes. Now here's a secret. Chandor has been working in secret on something my father doesn't even know about. And I don't want my father finding out about this. Chandor's created something that can neutralise Blueface," Celith replied.

"Ah, I see. Well, your secrets are safe with me as always. You can trust me not to tell your father. But what do you need me to do?"

"Can you have the royal guard keep an eye out for any suspicious package which arrives, just in case it might contain Blueface? Alert us at once if any such thing happens so we can deploy the neutralising chemical."

"You bet. But if that's all, why'd you want me to keep this a secret from your father?" Clour seemed a little puzzled.

"If my father knows that Chandor has created a neutralising agent for Blueface, Chandor must have tested it against Blueface. Which means Chandor is able to successfully create Blueface. We don't want my father to know that. We're afraid of the ramifications."

"Ah, I see." Clour's expression seemed to suggest that the implications had dawned on him. "Again, don't worry, both of you. Your secrets are safe with Uncle Clour." Clour gave them a wink.

~

The next few days passed tensely for Chandor and Celith while they waited to see if there would be any attempt on the king's life. Chandor and Celith monitored the news everyday.

"Chancellor Crull declares state of emergency in Clidurna and Lintal with his new powers; suspends both legislatures," read a news headline one day.

"Let's watch the video of it," said Celith to Chandor.

Chandor had his communicator play the holographic video.

"Chancellor Crull has declared a state of emergency in Clidurna and Lintal, with his newfound sovereignty over Lintal which was conferred on him by Acting President Lurth. With a state of emergency declared, Parliament in Clidurna and Congress in Lintal have been suspended. Despite protests by the opposition in both Clidurna and Lintal, Chancellor Crull firmly decreed that the legislatures would be suspended and that he would be granted sweeping emergency powers to arrest anyone suspected of suspicious activity."

A holographic Crull appeared. "Citizens of Clidurna and Lintal! It is with great regret that I have decided to announce a state of emergency in our lands. It is a decision I have made with a heavy heart, and I do not take the power entrusted to me by Acting President Lurth lightly. But this is the best decision in the face of the national security threat posed by the Blissaunean agent, Chandor, creator of the deadly substance which killed the leader of Clidurna's opposition. I know the opposition is not happy with this, but hear me out: this is for your safety. It was your leader who was murdered in cold blood, and I need these powers to seek justice. With these powers, I will eradicate the threat posed by Blissaune, the rogue agent Chandor and any of his associates who may be roaming these lands. I will keep Clidurna and Lintal safe."

"He must've been planning this all along," remarked Chandor.

"Or at least, as soon as you created Blueface," Celith chimed in.

"I've got to clear my name." Chandor exhaled heavily.

"But how?" asked Celith.

"I don't know, but I've got to get the message out to Clidurna and Lintal that it's not me who committed the murders, but Crull and goodness knows who else had helped him."

"But they won't believe you, especially if you're broadcasting from Blissaune."

"I know, that's why I'm racking my brains now to think of a solution," sighed Chandor.

~

It was not more than a few days before they received notice from Clour that something suspicious had cropped up.

"Celith! Your father's received a suspicious package. We don't know who it's from. Against our advice, he seems intent on opening it anyway."

"Quick, Chandor! There's no time to lose! It could be a package of Blueface!"

Chandor quickly grabbed a piece of his Meitnerium lunar breccia and put it in his pocket just in case it was Blueface in the package.

Chandor and Celith raced down to the palace to figure out what had just arrived. It could easily be an innocuous package, a false alarm. Still, they couldn't afford to take any chances with Crull being the way he was.

They dashed down the corridors, heart beating fast. Celith swore at her father under her breath, angry that he was always impulsive and dismissive of sound advice. It was just like him to want to open the package despite advice to the contrary. Indeed, it made him all the more determined to find out what was inside.

Breathless, they reached the entrance of the palace. They ran past the surprised guards and threw open the doors.

The king was sitting in his throne. He looked up, surprised. He was holding what looked like a small parcel in his hands.

"Father! Don't open it yet!" cried Celith.

The king shook his head dismissively and opened the package.

"NOOOO!!!" shouted Celith and Chandor in unison, running towards the king at the same time.

XI.   A hero

As the king opened the package, a fine dust filled the air. Before the kind realised what it was, the king began to cough profusely.

"His face is turning blue!" cried Celith. Celith began to cough too.

Before he knew it, Chandor began to cough incessantly as well. He knew at that moment that if he were to look in a mirror, his face would probably be turning blue too.

"Chandor! Quick!" Celith exclaimed in between coughs.

I don't want to die, thought Chandor.

Finding it difficult to concentrate while he was coughing badly, Chandor fumbled around. Finally, he found his lunar breccia in his pocket and threw it towards the king, right at the source of the Blueface that was dissipating into the air.

Nothing seemed to happen.

"Chan-ugh-dor. Help…" Celith continued to cough and was grabbing her throat.

Chandor was no better, trying to shield his mouth and nose with his hands, which was completely ineffective.

The king continued having a coughing fit and his face continued turning blue.

Then slowly but surely, the air seemed to clear. All of a sudden, the small moon dust particles in the air seemed to be attracted to the lunar breccia.

Celith's coughing got better.

Chandor's did as well.

The king still seemed to be coughing badly, but his face gradually regained its original colour.

Increasingly, more and more Blueface particles began to be attracted to the lunar breccia, until the movement of the particles in the air was visible and Chandor, Celith and the king saw them flying towards the lunar breccia.

Gradually, everybody stopped coughing.

"Chandor!" Celith squealed. "It worked!" Celith threw her arms around Chandor.

"My goodness, what just happened?" asked the king, still stunned.

"Chandor saved your life, father!" Celith answered.

"What? How?"

"You've just been the subject of an assassination attempt, Your Majesty. That was Blueface, what you've been trying to get me to create all this while," Chandor stated matter-of-factly.

"Hmph! Yes, I know, because you still haven't given me any of the Blueface I wanted."

"Well, I did something better. I created an antidote to Blueface. Well, it can't cure someone who's already breathed in too much Blueface, but if there's Blueface in the air, it can attract the Blueface to it and neutralise it." Chandor pointed at the lump near the throne. The lump, which originally looked glassy, now looked white like it was covered with snow, which was actually a result of absorbing the Blueface.

"He just saved your life, father," Celith reminded the king again.

"Well, I guess I certainly owe you, Chandor. But how did you create this antidote without having any Blueface around?"

"Well…I…" Chandor began.

"He's a genius, father. Let's not pretend to understand how geniuses work."

The king frowned, then smiled.

"I guess Celith is right. I won't put you in a spot, Chandor. You've saved my life after all. As the king of Blissaune, I will grant you 3 wishes. What do you want? Think hard before you answer me." The king laughed.

"I can think of the first one right now. First, stop making me create Blueface."

The king frowned again, but nodded. "Right. That's one wish. The other 2?"

Chandor thought for the moment and answered, "My communicator can't communicate with Clidurna and Lintal from within Blissaune. I want to make a broadcast to Clidurna and Lintal about what just happened today, and my whole story. I want to clear my name."

The king nodded again. "We can do that. What about your last wish?"

Chandor hesitated for a moment. He had a wild idea. He wondered whether he should ask for it or not.

Chandor was afraid how his idea would be taken. There was a very real chance it might backfire.

Oh, whyever not, thought Chandor. Throwing caution to the wind, he took a deep breath, then exhaled, before he went for broke.

"I want Celith's hand in marriage."

"What?" The king drew his breath in sharply.

"Chandor!" Celith squealed, delighted. She gave Chandor a tight hug, which Chandor returned.

"Well, I don't know," began the king.

"Father! Don't you think my happiness is important?" Celith asked the king.

"Of course, sweetheart, but are you sure? You barely know the man."

"I've spent many days with him in the lab, father. I can tell he is a man with principles and concern for the greater good of society. We've talked a lot more than many other people would in the same span of time. I know him well by now, father. And I hope you'll approve, because…" Celith looked shyly at Chandor, "I love him."

"Well…" the king stroked his chin thoughtfully.

"Very well, then. Chandor, I grant you my daughter's hand in marriage."

Chandor and Celith hugged each other. Chandor lifted Celith off the ground and swung her around in glee.

"We'll grant you a title, Chandor. You can't be marrying my daughter as a commoner. You shall henceforth be known as Duke Chandor."

"Most grateful, Your Majesty." Chandor did not care for the title, but he decided to be polite.

"So when do you want to do the broadcast to Lintal and Clidurna?"

"As soon as possible would be good."

"Right. Let's get to the broadcast studio and you'll be ready to go."

Chandor, Celith and the king left the palace and went down a series of hallways and corridors to the broadcast studio. It was a room with foam padding all over.

"Wow, it looks just like those television studios in the history books on earth," remarked Chandor. "When those things called televisions still existed."

"Well, it comes in handy when we need to broadcast something to Clidurna and Lintal. It doesn't rely on the network that your communicator relies on. In fact, it really is just like an old television station: it broadcasts using similar electromagnetic waves that people can tune in to," Celith chimed in.

"Now, we flick a switch, and then you're on in 5 seconds."

"We have to flick a real physical switch? It's not voice activated?" *Wow, Blissaune is really like a living museum*, thought Chandor.

"Yes, get ready," said the king. The king flicked a switch and gave Chandor a thumbs up.

Chandor took a deep breath, then began.

"Citizens of Clidurna and Lintal. My name is Chandor and I'm a chemical engineer.

I have been accused by Clidurna's Chancellor Crull of sabotage and murder. Nothing could be further from the truth. In fact, I have been framed by Crull. Crull is behind all of this.

I come from earth. My first stop on the moon was on Lintal. I was introduced by 2 persons on the spacecraft which I was on to Thurl, who was from Clidurna and worked for Lunasilico. Thurl offered me a job as he knew that I was a chemical engineer.

One day, there was some suspected sabotage from Blissaune. The police found me suspicious as I had just come from earth, but already seemed to know some people from Clidurna. To cut the long story short, I was kicked out of Lintal. In those circumstances, I accepted a job offer from Thurl to work at Lunasilico.

When I got to work at Lunasilico, I was tasked to find a cure for the inhalation of moon dust by harvester operators. Inadvertently, I stumbled upon something else instead. I discovered a new chemical which would cause the person or animal inhaling it to turn blue, choke, get silicosis and die. Blissaune has named this chemical Blueface.

Thurl let the head of Lunasilico, Svielyar, know about the chemical. Svielyar reported this to Crull. Crull ordered me to mass produce canisters of Blueface. I suspected something was amiss. Instead of producing Blueface, I delivered dummy canisters which would only cause a mild coughing fit.

I was proven right. The Leader of the Opposition in Clidurna took ill with a mild coughing fit soon thereafter. I knew that this was Crull's work, and that if I had provided Crull with the real Blueface, the Leader of the Opposition would have been killed then.

Crull had me arrested on suspicion of sabotage. He tried to have me sent for a psychiatric assessment to have me certified as mentally ill so that I wouldn't be able to tell my story in Court. However, before I could go for the psychiatric assessment, I was abducted by 2 troopers from Blissaune and brought to Blissaune.

In Blissaune, I found out that the Leader of the Opposition of Clidurna and the President of Lintal were dead, and they had turned blue in the face. There was no doubt in my mind that

Crull had killed them. Crull must have managed to have one of the chemical engineers in my former team concoct a batch of Blueface, which he then used to kill the Leader of the Opposition and the President of Lintal, so that he could declare a state of emergency and assume dictatorial powers.

The king of Blissaune had commissioned me to create Blueface for him. I did not want to do that. So, in secret, I instead began work on an antidote to Blueface. And I have found an almost-antidote. It attracts Blueface to itself, and if deployed quickly enough, it will save someone who's been exposed to Blueface.

Thankfully I did this. Today, there was an assassination attempt on the king of Blissaune. Someone sent him a package of Blueface. Fortunately, we managed to rush to the palace and deploy our antidote in the nick of time, just as I, Princess Celith and the king began to have a coughing fit.

I have no doubt at all that this latest assassination attempt is also engineered by Crull. Crull will stop at nothing to eliminate those who are opposed to him, to obtain ultimate power and control all of the moon. He already has control over Lintal and Clidurna, and now he wants to take over Blissaune too.

Citizens of Lintal and Clidurna, believe me. I am innocent, and I was framed by Crull. Crull must be stopped before more lives are lost."

Chandor signalled to the king to stop and the king flipped the physical switch off.

"Splendid, Chandor! So what do we do now that that's done?"

"We wait, I guess? And see whether the people of Lintal and Clidurna believe me or not. In the meantime, I think we've got a wedding to prepare for." Chandor smiled at the king.

~

Things moved fast after that. Chandor and Celith checked out the news the next day on Chandor's communicator.

"The protests in Lintal and Clidurna which began ever since Crull assumed emergency powers have gained a new momentum. Riots have rocked Lintal and Clidurna ever since a video was broadcast from Blissaune by a man named Chandor, a chemical engineer formerly from earth. Chandor claims that he was the original discoverer of the deadly chemical that killed the Leader of the Opposition of Clidurna and President of Lintal. According to Chandor, he was framed by Crull, who was the mastermind behind the murders, and who allegedly is doing so in order to gain emergency powers and control all of the moon. Citizens are demanding answers from Crull and claim that he is not speaking the truth."

"Looks like my speech had an effect," Chandor told Celith.

"It's too early to tell, though. Let's wait and see," Celith replied.

They did not have to wait long. The following day, there was another news broadcast with an even more dramatic turn of events.

"In the wake of the protests, in a surprising turn of events, Chancellor Crull has abandoned his post and left for earth. He was caught on camera taking a private spacecraft bound for earth yesterday night. Chancellor Crull has also broadcast a video of himself."

Crull's holographic face appeared through Chandor's communicator.

"Citizens of Clidurna and Lintal, I am Chancellor Crull. Over the past few days, there have been mounting protests over my emergency powers, and the broadcast by Chandor.

I maintain that I have done nothing wrong, and this latest attempt by Chandor is another instance of sabotage by Blissaune. Chandor is a Blissaunean agent, with the ulterior motive of destroying Lintal and Clidurna.

Nevertheless, with the protests escalating in intensity day by day, I fear for my personal safety. I am disappointed that many have chosen to believe Chandor instead of I. Things being what they are, I am relinquishing my post of Chancellor and I am leaving for earth."

The news on the communicator continued, "In view of Crull's departure, Lintal and Clidurna have separated again and now have 2 administrations, headed by a caretaker President and Chancellor respectively."

"Well, it seems like justice has been done," Chandor told Celith.

"Guess you saved the moon, didn't you?" Celith teased.

"Well, with Crull gone now, I guess I did, didn't I? Things could have turned out a lot worse." Chandor grinned at Celith.

A trooper came into the room, interrupting them.

"We have a special transmission for you from Clidurna, Duke Chandor. You'll need to head over to the broadcast studio."

Chandor and Celith headed over to the broadcast studio, wondering what this latest news might be. Once they entered the broadcast studio, the trooper flicked a switch, and the holograms of Thurl and Svielyar appeared before them.

"Chandor. It's good to see you again. I want you to know that I've always believed in you, even if I had not suspected Crull of wrongdoing," began Thurl.

"It's good to see you too, Chandor," Svielyar joined in.

"I'm pleased to see you again too, Thurl and Svielyar. I've got Princess Celith of Blissaune here with me as well." Chandor gestured at Celith.

"Pleased to make your acquaintance, Princess Celith," Svielyar continued, "Well, Chandor, as you know, Crull has abandoned his post as Chancellor. Though I still don't know exactly what happened, changes are certainly afoot here in Clidurna. I've just been appointed a minister in the new government by emergency decree, and in the meantime Thurl is now the acting head of Lunasilico. Thurl has given a strong recommendation about you to the caretaker Chancellor and vouched for your innocence. The caretaker Chancellor would like to invite you back to Clidurna to participate in our new government. In particular, he wants to normalise trading ties with Blissaune and thinks you could help there."

Chandor shook his head. "Nope. Sorry."

"May I ask why?"

"I'm getting married to Celith, so I'm going to have to stay in Blissaune."

Thurl laughed. "Well, if you aren't an amazing man, Chandor. You amazed me at how quickly you adapted to moon life, then being uprooted from Lintal to Clidurna without missing a beat. And now you're settling down in Blissaune and even marrying their princess! While I'm sad for Clidurna's loss, I'm happy for you. Congratulations."

"You have my congratulations too, Chandor. It's a pity we can't have you back in Clidurna, but I guess you've already decided to settle down in Blissaune," said Svielyar.

"Thank you for the congratulations, everyone," said Chandor.

~

Chandor and Celith's wedding preparations got into full swing. As they were working out some details in the palace, the king came to them.

"Alright, my favourite daughter," the king said to Celith.

"You mean, your only daughter," Celith rolled her eyes.

"That's the same thing. Well, what do you want for your wedding gift?"

Celith thought long and hard. Then she gave an unexpected answer to the king.

"I want you to democratise Blissaune. Have democratic elections, and let Blissaune be run by the people's elected representatives. Let Blissaune be a constitutional monarchy."

"What?!" The king choked as if he had just inhaled Blueface.

"I hope you respect my wishes, father. I'm actually a member of the Democratic Activists League. You never knew about it. But it was to protect you as well. I was a force of moderation in the Democratic Activists League. I don't want you to come to harm, and I don't want some of the more extreme members to hurt you. Transitioning to a constitutional monarchy is just about the mildest and most reasonable proposal there is."

Chandor felt the need to speak up for Celith. "Your Majesty, it's understandable that you're upset. But you cannot doubt Celith's loyalty and love for you. Celith and I saved you when you were nearly going to die from Blueface. This is also the best way to save the monarchy and avoid the possibility of a revolution by those in the Democratic Activists League who see you as evil personified."

"Will you give this to me as a wedding gift, father?"

The king stared at Celith, then at Chandor, then at Celith again.

"Well, you know what? I think my precious daughter is right. I promise, I'll give it a try, for your sake. You have my word that I'll have elections held for a prime minister and Blissaune will be governed democratically from now on."

Celith and Chandor whooped with joy.

"I guess you haven't just saved the moon, you've saved Blissaune as well," Celith told Chandor.

"Not me. Us." Chandor leaned in and gave Celith a kiss.

XII.   Epilogue

It was as romantic a setting as a wedding on the moon could be. Chandor and Celith were in a glass dome, from which the sky could be seen. They picked a special day on which there would be a sunset on this location on the moon. The dome was filled with well-wishers, including ordinary citizens of Blissaune, holders of noble titles, and now, the democratically elected Prime Minister and Cabinet of Blissaune.

"I pronounce you man and wife. You may now kiss the bride," the officiant declared, using the words of an age-old tradition developed on earth.

Just as it was in the old days on earth, Celith wore a flowing, lacy white gown, with a white veil and Chandor wore a tuxedo.

Chandor drew back the veil, leaned in, and kissed Celith deeply.

The crowd erupted in cheers.